THE DEVIL IN DETAIL

THE DEVIL IN DETAIL

AN ODYSSEY IN THE SURREAL

BRIAN STABLEFORD

WILDSIDE PRESS

For the Devil,
to whom, although he does not exist, I owe more than
I can possibly repay, given the mediocre quality of my soul.

CHAPTER I

It was in 1997—which now seems a long time ago, although it wasn't, in terms of the Great Cosmic Clock—that I made my formal pact with the Devil. I stress the word *formal* because, as Oswald Spengler pointed out in *The Decline of the West*, we now life in a Faustian Age in which the entire culture in which we exist has made a tacit pact with the Devil, within whose terms we all live. I was aware of that prior to 1997 but until then I had not actually had the opportunity to make the Devil's acquaintance, and had assumed, given his non-existence, at least in the sense in which "existence" is commonly understood, that I never would. I was, however, wrong about that, and the purpose of writing this down now, nearly twenty years after the event, is to explain the peculiar circumstances in which it came about, and the consequences that the advantages of hindsight now allow me to see.

I did not write or give anyone an account of what happened at the time—at least not an accurate one—because I suspected that they might consider me insane if I did so. I was not entirely certain myself that I was not, in spite of the Devil's assurances to the contrary, and his seemingly-reasonable explanations for his true nature and my ability to encounter him and make a pact with him in spite of his "non-existence." I still cared about my image in those days, but I am now an old age pensioner, and the government does not stop paying you a pension merely because you are generally deemed to be insane, or, indeed, if you actually are.

There are still reasons that perhaps ought to inhibit me slightly. I was for a brief while a part-time teacher of creative writing on an M.A. course in "Writing for Children" at what was then King Alfred's College, Winchester, and I was always careful to tell my students that, although there were absolutely no rules of writing, despite what Elmore Leonard might think, I felt obliged to give them two excellent pieces of advice, the first of which was never write to anything autobiographical (the second, in case anyone is interested, was never write a story about bullying).

Neither item of advice was received kindly by my students, but my explanation for the first one was that fiction ought to consist of honest lies, and autobiography, whether fictionalized or not, inevitably consists of dishonest lies. "As Winston Churchill said," I used to misquote, "there are lies, damn, lies, statistics, history and autobiography." If anyone objected, as someone occasionally did, that dictionaries of quotations tend to suspend the list with "statistics," I explained that that was because historians had censored the fourth term, and that the fifth had been dropped because nobody likes to think that all possible accounts of their own lives—especially the one that consciousness and memory unscrupulously render to them by way of supplying them with a notion of identity—are actually mere tissues of distortions, inventions and self-serving hypocrisies.

So, if I were still prepared to practice now what I preached then, I ought not to be writing this story at all, but at least I can be upfront now in admitting, right from the outset, that whereas most of my works of fiction are absolutely honest lies, this one will probably a little bit suspect. The reasons for that will probably be fairly obvious already, but they will doubtless become clearer in the progress of the narrative, in the course of which I not only make my pact with the supposedly-non-existent Devil but also make fleeting contact with the thesis to which he is the logical antithesis, the Creator, alias the Cosmic Mind, whose non-existence is generally considered to be more debatable.

Anyway, I believed at the time, and still believe, that I made the relevant pact and the contact in question, although, as a dyed-in-the-wool skeptic, I naturally mistrust everything that I believe. If that seems paradoxical, and hence unacceptable to the commonsensical reader, it merely serves to demonstrate the awful extent to which Aristotelian logic has taken root in our culture, in spite of the fact that we all know perfectly well, thanks to Werner Heisenberg, that the physical world really is paradoxical. Nowadays, no one with a nodding acquaintance with the enigma of Schrödinger's Cat can reasonable refuse to believe that things can both exist and not exist at the same time—or, at the very least, ought to be prepared to both believe it and not believe it, in a scrupulously undiscriminatory fashion.

So, at least for the sake of the narrative, the reader ought to be prepared to believe that the Devil, like Schrödinger's famous feline while still in the sealed box, both exists and does not exist. Ditto the Creator, and the narrative voice, alias me. It really ought not to be difficult, given that such stubborn paradoxicality really is the way of the physical world as well as the world of fiction.

In any case, a person who has made a formal pact with the Devil surely owes it to posterity to make a record of the terms of the pact in question, even if he did not actually sign it in blood, for the sake of the moral annals of humankind, and even if those annals only have a few years to run before civilization collapses and books become extinct, along with animals and people.

In addition, the Devil told me himself to publish and be damned, and I really wouldn't like to disappoint him, as he was such a likeable fellow.

The Cosmic Mind won't care either way, of course, having too many other things to worry about.

So here goes.

I was putting the final touches to the introduction to a new edition of C. D. Pamely's *Tales of Mystery and Terror* for a small press publisher when the phone rang. I picked it up with my left hand while my right forefinger finished pecking out the last few words of the sentence.

"Hello."

"Brian? Lionel, Cardiff."

Lionel Fanthorpe rarely uses his surname when identifying himself to his friends in outward calls, preferring his place of residence.

"Hi, Lionel," I said, attempting—unavailingly, of course—to match the cheerfulness and ebullience of his tone. "How's fame treating you?"

In 1997 Lionel had recently achieved a measure of celebrity by virtue of being appointed the presenter of *Fortean TV*, a magazine program devoted to the not-entirely earnest investigation of weird events and individuals. This had caused a certain amount of controversy in the broadsheet press, some of whose columnists had thought it unbecoming of a minister of the Church of Wales to lend his clerical collar to such irreverence.

"It's marvelous," he assured me. "Actually, that's why I'm ringing you."

"You want me to appear on *Fortean TV*?" If I sounded skeptical, it's because I am—and it's because I was universally renowned for my skepticism in those days that I had every right to be skeptical about the possibility of ever being invited to appear on *Fortean TV*.

"Oh, no—sorry, but we're already nearly full up for the next series. Ever since the first series aired I've been deluged with calls from all kinds of people clamoring to get on. You wouldn't believe some of the stories they tell."

"Actually, Lionel," I said, "I wouldn't believe any of the stories they tell—but I do believe that you've been deluged with calls. What do you expect if you set yourself up as the front man for rent-a-crank?"

"That's exactly why I thought you might be useful in the present circumstance, if not as a contributor to *Fortean TV*," he told me, refusing to take the slightest offence. Lionel's geniality knows no bounds; he is the most admirable man I know.

"What present circumstance is that?" I enquired.

"The publicity generated by the show has led to my receiving other requests and proposals," he explained, beating around the bush somewhat. "It's because Martin saw an episode of the show that he got in touch, but he wanted to consult me in my official capacity. He wants me to exorcise a supernatural presence in his bookshop."

"Do you perform exorcisms?" I asked, having previously assumed that that was a prerogative of the Catholic clergy and African witch-doctors.

"It's not something I do lightly," he assured me, "but if I'm convinced that it will do some good, I'm prepared to employ any of the Church's rituals. I believe that exorcism is a legitimate weapon in the war against evil."

Lionel is what the Victorians would have described as a *muscular Christian*—not so much because he has a black belt in judo as because he believes that the power of active evil has to be countered by an equal and opposite reaction. He is the only man I know who could say "Praise the Lord and pass the ammunition!" with perfect sincerity.

"Why do you need me?" I said. "The presence of a strident atheist is hardly likely to help the party go with a bang. Assuming, of course, that departing demons do go with a bang, as well as the obligatory whiff of brimstone."

"I wouldn't need you for the exorcism, even if there is one," said Lionel, cheerily, "but I feel obliged to mount a preliminary investigation first, in order to try to determine whether there really is some kind of supernatural presence in the shop, and whether, if so, it's demonic. A skeptic might be useful, to add balance to the committee of investigation."

"Committee?" I queried.

"Oh, just three of us. I've invited another of my acquaintances along to provide her expertise."

"And what expertise is that?" I asked, skeptically.

"She's a leading member of the local branch of the Society for Psychical Research Society."

My relentlessly antiquarian mind inevitably associates the SPR with its Victorian heyday, and the investigations of Katie King and D. D. Home mounted by the likes of William Crookes and Oliver Lodge. I was aware, however, that it was still going strong in 1997—and, indeed, still is, proudly proclaiming on its website the admirable fundamental aim of examining "without prejudice or prepossession and in a scientific spirit those faculties of man, real or supposed, which appear to be inexplicable on any generally recognized hypothesis."

"It's not something of which I have any experience," I confessed, dutifully, although the prospect of joining an investigative committee to evaluate a possible haunting was an intriguing possibility.

"I know," he said, "but I thought you might be qualified, and interested enough to sit in on a preliminary investigation—an all-night sitting—so that we can try to figure out exactly what we're dealing with. I read your thing in Steve's anthology."

"Ah," I said, as a measure of enlightenment dawned. Steve Jones had edited an anthology for Gollancz which consisted of famous horror writers' true encounters with the supernatural. Not wishing to miss out on the opportunity for a sale, in spite of never having had any such encounter, in the commonly understood sense, I had supplied a piece wittily entitled "*Chacun sa goule*" which had offered a scrupulously accurate account of a real event: the coincidental discovery of a rare book by Maurice Maeterlinck at an antiquarian book fair, which I had stumbled across by chance. Typically, I had supplemented my record of the bare facts with a philosophical rhapsody about the existential significance of the continued permeation of the world by the carbonaceous matter that once made up the bodies of the dead. I had observed that the carbon dioxide in every breath we take contains atoms that might once have been part of the people of the past, whose minds also echo in the pages of their writings, so that the dead do indeed retain a "ghostly" presence in the present. Although graveyards are doubtless replete with such ghosts, I had said in the article, the most significant of my own "ghostly encounters" invariably took place in bookshops, involving contact with the ghosts of authors via the presence of their works.

It was perhaps not unnatural, therefore, that on being told about a haunted bookshop—a bookshop whose resident supernatural presence was so discomfiting as perhaps to require exorcism—Lionel might think of me.

"Well?" said Lionel. "Are you interested?"

"What bookshop?" I parried. "Where?"

"It's a second-hand place—just down the coast, in Barry."

"There isn't a second-hand bookshop in Barry," I said, confidently. I had previously lived in Swansea for several years and had continued to visit my children there for several more years when the Ex moved back there after deserting me. If there had been a second-hand bookshop in Barry, I would have found mention of it in *drif's guide* and made every effort to visit it.

"It hasn't been there long," Lionel told me.

"And it's haunted already? By whom?"

"Martin's not sure that it's the premises that are haunted. He thinks it might be the books."

I nearly came out with some facetious crack about Martin presumably having picked up a copy of Abdul Alhazred's *Necronomicon* at a jumble sale in Tiger Bay, but I hesitated. The idea of haunted books was not without a certain appeal—in fact, the mere mention of books was inevitably appealing to a person of the kind that I was then, who lived in a five-bedroomed house in which every brick wall was covered with books and who had commissioned a friend who was a builder to construct two garages in the back garden in order to contain the thousands of books that wouldn't fit in the house.

It's all gone now, of course; I had to get rid of the books and the house when **** deserted me in her turn, and I now live in one room with hardly any books at all—both circumstances that help to make the pension go a lot further—but in those days, a chance to visit a second-hand bookshop that I hadn't visited before was like Camembert on the spike of a mousetrap to me.

Even the newest second-hand bookshop, I knew, needed old books to dress its shelves. Some people anxious to move into the trade back in the twentieth century, when there still was a trade, used their own collections as bases, but hardened collectors were usually so reluctant to put out their old favorites that they would shop around instead for anything that could be bought in bulk at a reasonable price.

I knew that there had been a time in the nineteenth century when the coal industry was booming and Cardiff had been a busy port. The burgeoning middle class had had aspirations in those days—C. D. Pamely's father had been a mining engineer in Pontypridd but he'd harbored greater ambitions for his sons—and it was possible that there were some nice caches of good antiquarian stock lurking in a place like Barry, which had been a haven for the south Wales gentry before slipping way down-market to become a third-rate holiday resort. Haunted or not, therefore, there was a slim possibility that the mysterious Martin's shop might have some interesting contents—and if it had opened too recently to obtain an entry in the latest issue of *drif,* the professional vultures might not have had the chance to strip the shelves clean of tasty meat.

There is nothing that gladdens the heart of an obsessive book-accumulator like the thought of virgin stock, and although my obsessive tendencies had not yet reached their present magnificent orderliness back in 1997, they were pretty forceful.

"It sounds very interesting," I said to Lionel, effortlessly switching into earnest mode. "When do you propose to hold this investigative vigil?"

"Monday," said Lionel.

It was short notice, but I assumed that it would have been even shorter if Lionel hadn't been otherwise occupied on Sundays.

"Suits me," I said, firmly hooked and avid to be reeled in. "Name your time and place, and I'll be there. I'm looking forward to it already."

CHAPTER II

Lionel picked me up from Cardiff station in an old Cortina whose funereal paint job seemed appropriate to the occasion. He already had two passengers in place so I had no choice but to take a back seat. There wasn't a lot of space for me, let alone my overnight bag, but I squeezed myself in.

"This is Martin," Lionel said, indicating the middle-aged man whose claim to the front seat had obviously been secured by reason of dimension as well as opportunity, "and this is Penny, from the local Society for Psychical Research."

"Presumably not a full-time employee?" I quipped, nodding politely to a thin, thirty-ish woman with spectacles whose lenses were almost as powerful as mine.

The bespectacled woman did not seem to appreciate the flippancy of my tone, and might even have failed momentarily in her duty to regard me without prejudice or prepossession. "No," she said, in a severe manner which suggested that she'd been warned about my skeptical tendencies.

It was left to Lionel to supplement the blunt denial. "Penny works for the Welsh Development Agency," he said.

"Awdurdod Datblygu Cymru," she corrected. Having been married to the Ex, I knew that she was merely translating the term into Welsh, presumably being a member of the Welsh Language Society—or Cymdeithas yr Iaith Gymraeg, as she would presumably put it. The lilt of her accent inevitably came out fully in the way that she pronounced the phrase.

"My ex-wife works for the Welsh Development Agency," I said, trying to win a little moral credit, although I couldn't actually inject any enthusiasm into the term "my ex-wife" and the comment might have sounded more like an insult than I'd intended. Penny's answering stare did not suggest that the revelation had won me any sympathy.

"Penny's done postgrad research at Duke," said Lionel, trying heroically to overcome the momentary awkwardness as the car pulled way into the last remnants of the rush-hour traffic, "in the selfsame labs where J. B. Rhine once worked." He sounded as if that qualification alone ought to be sufficient to demand my reverence.

"I thought you could do that sort of thing in the UK now," I said. "Didn't Arthur Koestler leave a bequest to set up an established chair in paranormal studies? Somebody took the money in the end, didn't they?"

"There isn't a course here," the woman explained. "I wanted to do a proper course."

I didn't want to offend her further by challenging her use of the word "proper". Instead I cast an appraising eye over the equipment with which she had surrounded herself. I recognized the fancy temperature tracking-gauge and the video camera easily enough, but most of the rest was in leather cases, and it wasn't obvious what the ammeter on her knee was supposed to be connected to.

"So we're the whole investigative committee, are we?" I commented, carefully refraining from making any reference to *Ghostbusters*.

"We are," Lionel confirmed. "If Penny picks up anything interesting, of course, she'll call in some of her associates for a more thorough investigation—with Martin's permission, that is."

The way that he added the qualifying clause made me wonder whether Martin's permissiveness might already have been severely tested by Lionel's insistence that a preliminary investigation would be necessary before deciding whether an exorcism might be required. I could understand why that might be the case; even though the traditional silly season wouldn't be under way for another two months, the *Fortean Times* was hot enough nowadays to have all its best stories followed up by the *Sun* and the *Daily Star*, not to mention the *Sunday Sport*, which still existed back in 1997. That kind of coverage might boost the clientele of a haunted bookshop for a week or two, but the embarrassment might last a lifetime. I assumed that what Martin had had in mind when he first approached Lionel had not included an investigative committee or the possibility of a full-scale SPR investigation.

Indeed, the bookshop-proprietor was quick to chip in. "I hope the reverend explained to you, Mr. Stableford," he intoned, in a broad way-up-the-valleys accent, "that this whole business is confidential."

"No one will hear a whisper of it from me," I assured him. "My lips are sealed with superglue."

I can be very pedantic when giving out promises; while I am typing this page, not a sound is escaping from my lips.

"Perhaps you could begin filling Brian and Penny in on the background details while we're on the road, Martin," Lionel suggested. "It will give them some idea of what to expect."

Martin did not seem overjoyed by this prospect. In fact, he looked as if he might be having second thoughts about the wisdom of having approached Lionel in the first place, but the incumbent at his local chapel was unlikely to do exorcisms, or to look kindly upon anyone who broached the possibility. The great majority of Welsh Methodists tend to the view that a man who imagines himself to be troubled by ghosts or demons is, *ipso facto*, a man with an unusually guilty conscience, who should look deep into his own soul for the source of his disquiet.

I must admit that I tended to agree at the time, and I still do, in spite of what happened to me during and after my sojourn in Martin's haunted bookshop, and what it might be taken to imply about the state of my own conscience.

"Would you rather I did it?" Lionel asked, when Martin was slow to accept his invitation, his enthusiasm to hold forth being as boundless as his geniality. Lionel is not a man of few words, but, on the plus side, he is never boring. I have not actually been to his church since he kindly invited me to his ordination, but I am prepared to bet that his parishioners get full value from his sermons.

"No," said Martin, his mind quickly made up. "Best if…well, see, I'm from the Rhondda originally. In the industry till the last pits closed—not a face worker, mind, always above ground. Middle management, I suppose, is the phrase they use nowadays. Anyhow, I was over twenty years in when the ax finally came down, an' the redundancy was a nice package. I'm only forty-three, so I knew I had to use the money sensibly—start a business, like. Well, I'd always been a reader, an' it just so happened that I was still in the office, tidying up, when one of the old boys we'd kept on to do the clearing up came in to ask what we wanted done with all the books from the old colliery library.

"I didn't even know there'd ever been a colliery library, but when the boys had found all these boxes of books in a storage-loft, the old-timer had recognized them—said he'd often seen the like around his house in the old days, when his father and grandfather had been regular borrowers. It had fallen into disuse in the fifties, I suppose, what with paperbacks an' all, an' the room it was in had been turned into an office. So I said: 'It's all right, boys, I'll look after those—put what you can into my car, and pile the rest up in the bike-sheds. I'll ferry the boxes home a few at a time.' Well, nobody else wanted them, did they?

"I thought at first I'd just look through them, like—sort out anything I wanted to read and give the rest to Oxfam—but when I got the old boy to help me stow the second batch he said that if I'd got a good home, he knew where the books from the old Workingmen's Institute had been put away when they turned it into a club an' the library was turfed out in favor of a snooker table. That's when I got the idea. Ours couldn't have been the only pit in Wales with its own library, nor our village the only one with a Workingmen's Institute, an' we're not the kind of folk to throw things away. Why not scout around, I thought, see what I can dig up, an' open a bookshop?"

Why not indeed? I thought, sympathetically.

"I knew there was no point doing something like that in the valley, mind," Martin continued, "or even in Merthyr. I thought of Caerleon first, but the wife wasn't happy about moving to what's practically England, an' I knew Cardiff already had two second-hand bookshops, so I thought of Barry, which the wife has always liked because she used to go on holiday to the Island when she was a girl. It turned out that a lot of stuff from the old colliery libraries had been sold years ago to old Ralph in Swansea or to that shop that used to be in the Hayes before it all got torn down, but I found half a dozen more sizeable lots that I picked up for next to nothing and a couple of smaller ones."

"How many books altogether?" I asked, impatient for hard news of some practical relevance.

"About twelve thousand, give or take, although some of them, quite honestly, are so filthy that they're only fit for putting on the fire. Make a nice blaze, mind, as most of the dirt is coal dust."

It wasn't as big a total as I'd hoped. Given the educational mission of nineteenth century Workingmen's Institutes, I guessed that at least half the books would probably be practical non-fiction, now hopelessly out of date, and half the rest would probably be religious texts. Even if there were only three thousand volumes of fiction, however, I calculated swiftly—and even if the bulk of those were standard sets of Scott and Dickens, there ought to be something of interest. In all probability, none of the books would have seen the light of day for at least twenty years, and some might not have been inspected for the best part of a century—and the most exciting fact of all was that Martin didn't seem to have a clue about the book trade. In a business full of sharks, he gave the impression of being pure whitebait.

"How long, exactly, has the shop been open for business?" I asked.

"Open for business?" Martin echoed, incredulously. "It hasn't been open at all. Didn't the reverend…?"

"Sorry, Martin," Lionel interposed. "When I phoned Brian I didn't realize that you hadn't got that far."

My heart was still busy leaping by that point. Not just virgin stock but extra virgin stock, untouched by sharkish fin!

"Do you think," Penny put in, the musical quality of her accent covering up the slight hint of resentment, "that we could get on to the paranormal activity?"

I had quite forgotten, in my collector's excitement, that Martin's was supposed to be a *haunted* bookshop. I couldn't help remembering J. W. Dunne's theory that ghosts are really images displaced in the fourth dimension, from parallel worlds where time might be running ahead of or behind our own, and considering the whimsical possibility that Martin's as-yet-unopened bookshop might be haunted by the shades of dozens of book dealers resident in neighboring worlds in the multiverse, who had been dreaming about the virgin bookshop and contemplating it in a covetous spirit.

"Yes," I said, trying to sound politely supportive of our collective mission. "Tell us about the ghosts."

"I never said *ghosts*," said Martin, his voice suddenly infected by a note of pedantic caution. "I never saw a *person*, you understand. Whatever it is, I'm sure it's not *people*." He seemed oddly insistent, inevitably suggesting that someone else—his wife, perhaps?—had jumped to the conclusion that the haunter *was* a person.

"Poltergeist phenomena, then?" said Penny, eagerly. "Books moving by themselves—pages turning? Or is it a matter of sudden chills, changes in atmosphere?"

"Bit of the shivers, like," Martin conceded. "Wouldn't mind, if it were only that—cold, creaking an' so on."

"So what is it, exactly?" Penny wanted to know.

"Don't know, exactly. You're the expert, I suppose—you an' the reverend. I didn't notice anything at first—even the wife thought the place was all right, when it was empty. It's a lock-up, of course; we weren't planning on living there although it's got what the estate agent called living accommodation on the first floor. Modern family couldn't live there, even if their kids had long gone—too small by half, an' the bathroom facilities are woefully inadequate, not much more than an old sink and a cracked mirror. I decided to use the so-called bedroom as a second stock-room, put shelves in an' everything. Plan was that when I'd got the shop going steady, we'd both move down to Barry, to a nice house overlooking the sea, but there's not much chance of that now, until it's properly sorted—by the reverend, I mean. It's not so bad in daylight, of course, but even then…well, the wife's only been in there by day, an' she swears she'll never set foot in it again, even at high noon. I've been in there past midnight, putting up the shelves—but only the once, since I started putting out the stock. Seems to me as if the *presence* came with the stock, like, although it wasn't there when the books were all in boxes piled up in my garage back home. It's a real mystery."

"If it were a single haunted book," Lionel mused, "you might be able to solve the problem just by getting rid of that one volume."

"If it is," said Martin, darkly, "an' you can figure out which one, you can have it for nothing."

Given his account of how he'd acquired his stock, Martin could probably afford to be generous. Given that his stock had been on the shelves of private lending libraries for many years, however—and then stored in various lofts and cupboards for many years more—presumably without anyone complaining about any kind of haunting, it was difficult to see how the problem could be one of the books, or even all of them.

My preliminary judgment, inevitably, was that the problem was probably in Martin's mind. If he'd lived most of his life in the Rhondda, I thought, and only moved away when he was transferred to other pits as the industry faded away, the prospect of starting a new life in Barry must be a trifle daunting. In effect, he was one of the last surviving heirs of hundreds of years of mining tradition, and having spent all his own working life in the industry, it could hardly be easy to confront the terrible wrench of entry into an alien way of life. Reader or not, he was obviously no connoisseur; he'd seen an opportunity of sorts and he'd felt obliged to seize it, but he must have thought himself caught between the devil of new endeavor and the deep blue sea of unemployment. Was it so very surprising that the devil in question had indeed turned, in his fearful mind, into a tangible force of darkness?

Lionel was still following his own train of thought. "What kind of book might that be, do you think?" he asked, of no one in particular. For a moment, I thought he was really going to bring up the *Necronomicon*, but he took the second worst option. "A grimoire, maybe? A copy of the *Key of Solomon*?"

"Sure," I said, sarcastically. "Every colliery in the valley used to have its resident wizard, who kept his secret lore on the top shelf of the library, bound up to look like records of coal-production. You shift sixteen tons, and what do you get? Another day older an' deeper in debt. Jesus don't you call me, 'cause I can't go—I owe my soul to the pithead whore." I was content to recite the words with only the faintest lilt; I have the singing voice of a crow with laryngitis.

"Actually," said Penny, showing not the slightest sign of sympathy with my jocular attitude, "it wasn't unknown for eighteenth century mines, and even for early factories, to have luckmen—wizards of a sort. Miners tended to be extremely very superstitious. It was a high-risk industry, you see. The transition from forced labor to wage-labor wasn't as long ago as you might think, even in these parts, and the transition from superficial workings—actual *pits*, that is—to deep shaft mining was a step into unknown territory, which took them further and further into a dark underworld. Then again, the communities were often small and insular, not only prone to develop their own eccentric legends and traditions, but heavily dependent on their elders and opinion-makers. The activities of the luckmen would have been vital to the morale of their fellow-workers."

"Did they teach you all that at Duke?" I asked, in a neutral tone.

"No," she said. "The LSE. I did a degree in sociology before I did my master's in parapsychology."

That probably explained, I thought, how she'd landed a job with the Welsh Development Agency, which was notorious as a feather-bed for the educated wing of what the contemptuous English called the Taffia. Not that I was at all dismissive of the LSE or sociology; I'd been a lecturer in sociology myself at the University of Reading for twelve years before I quit to write full-time. I'd never heard of luckmen and was routinely suspicious of the Welsh mythology and legendry that had mostly been artificially generated in the nineeetnth century, but in fairness, I'd done my first degree in biology, so I'd never studied industrial sociology at all.

"And were these luckmen in the habit of consulting books of protective rituals?" I asked, trying to maintain a scrupulously neutral tone of voice.

"I don't know," she said.

"If they did," Lionel put in, "moving the book might have been the crucial disturbance—like moving bones laid to eternal rest. Didn't M. R. James once say that all his stories were variations on the theme of *curst be he who moves my bones*?"

"If it's a case of *curst be him who moves my books*," I opined, reverting to type in spite of my resolution to treat the business seriously, "we're more likely to be dealing with a dyed-in-the-wool book-collector than a black magician. I'd come back to haunt anyone who creased the dust-wrapper on one of mine. Hell hath no fury like a collector who finds a shopping-list scribbled on a flyleaf."

Lionel laughed, probably to be polite. Neither of the others cracked a smile. It looked as if it was going to be a long night, but I consoled myself with the knowledge that I could keep myself busy for hours with that much stock. Fool that I was, I had no inkling of the horrible shock that was to come as we pulled up outside the bookshop and climbed out of the car.

CHAPTER III

Martin's shop wasn't in a prime position, even by Barry's standards, but it was close enough to the seafront to catch a certain amount of passing trade during the holiday season. He was enough of a businessman to realize that his bread-and-butter business would be selling paperback pulp to people who needed something to occupy their eyes while they lay around after exhausting the so-called pleasures of the so-called Pleasure Park, so the wooden shelves he'd erected in the window were stocked with former best-sellers that looked as if they'd been culled from all the charity shops in south Wales.

When Martin unlocked the front door Penny and Lionel had enough respect for the alleged supernatural presence to pause for a moment, so I was first in. Although the sun hadn't set, it was hidden by the houses on the far side of the street and the window display blocked out most of the light that was left, so I had to wait for Martin to switch on the electric light before I could actually set to work. It wasn't until the light came on and I had a good look round—I could still do that in 1997 although my eyesight had already begun to go west—that the full appalling horror of the situation hit me.

I shouldn't have been surprised, of course, but rampant acquisitiveness generates the kind of optimism that sometimes allows inconvenient realizations to slip through the cracks of consciousness. One steady connoisseur sweep of my gaze across the shelves on the back wall was sufficient to tell me what I should have guessed the moment Martin started going on about old colliery libraries and the innate reluctance of honest folk to throw anything away. Maybe if his name had been Hywel or Dai the awful datum would have clicked into place, but Martin is an English name, and that had somehow taken priority in my preconceptions over the fact that his accent was broadest valley-speak.

Alas, many of the books he'd picked up for "next to nothing"—perhaps even the majority of them—were in Welsh.

What Martin had managed to acquire probably wasn't the entire stock of the old libraries, I realized, but merely that fraction of it that had been left behind when the readily-saleable stuff had gone. Even at first glance, it was obvious that it mostly consisted of texts whose utilitarian worth had been severely compromised by the fact that they were printed in a language falling swiftly into disuse south of Gwynedd, in spite of the heroic efforts of Cymdeithas yr Iaith Gymraeg.

If the bookshop really is haunted, I thought, bitterly, *the culprit is more likely to be a dead language than a dead person.*

"Do you get many Welsh speakers in Barry?" I asked, mournfully.

"Welsh is taught in all the schools," Martin said, proudly. "Legal requirement, see. Not so many speak it at home nowadays, of course, except up north—but people from Gwynedd and Clwyd go on holiday like anyone else. Can't keep a language alive without books, can you?"

By this time I had quick-scanned all eight of the shelves against the back wall and had turned my attention to the books behind the desk where the ancient cash-register stood. Most dealers keep their best stock—or what they think of as their best stock—behind their own station, in order to minimize the risk of theft. Not all the books behind the cash-register were in Welsh, but sixty per cent of them were, and the rest were evenly divided between books on mining and religious texts. That seemed to me to be a sad comment on Martin's judgment of saleability as well as his stock.

"Didn't the library stock include any English literature?" I asked him, plaintively. "Or any illustrated books, perhaps?"

"Some," Martin conceded. "I put the old fiction upstairs. That's standard practice, isn't it?" He'd obviously done a little market research and observed that most second-hand book dealers relegated the dross of ancient best-sellers and book club editions to the remotest corner they had. My spirits recovered a little; it was in such neglected corners that I always found my best bargains: rare works of nineteenth or early twentieth-century fantasy whose specialist significance was unappreciated by run-of-the-mill bookfairies or dealers whose own particular expertise was in railway books, natural history or whatever.

"The luckmen would have been Welsh speakers, of course," observed Penny, who was bringing in her second load of equipment and supplies while Lionel went back to the car for the remainder. "All their spells and incantations would have been handed down from time immemorial."

"They must have been true descendants of Myrddin Wyllt and Owain Glyndwr, mustn't they?" I put in, insouciantly, imagining the correct spelling in my head although I made no attempt to pronounce the names with an authentic Welsh diction. "The last custodians of the great Druidic tradition."

She looked at me as if I were half a caterpillar that she'd just discovered in a salad sandwich, evidently suspecting that I was being sarcastic. "Yes," she said, simply. "That's exactly what they were."

Diplomacy compelled me to refrain from making any clever remarks about Taliesin, the Bardic motto, Eisteddfods or male voice choirs, let alone the Taffia. I also refrained from making any observations about the apparent lack of any uncanny presence, for the moment, although I glanced at Martin while Penny went back outside to check that Lionel had ferried all of her kit inside.

Martin looked a trifle uncomfortable, but I suspected that it was because he found the situation directly embarrassing. I was now fully convinced that he'd approached Lionel in the hope of getting a quick, discreet and effective exorcism carried out without anyone else finding out about it. Not knowing Lionel, he had failed to calculate the abundance of enthusiasm that had not only brought in the reinforcement of the Society for Psychical Research but some skeptical smartarse who was probably immune to all supernatural malaise.

Dutifully, I resumed scanning the supposed cream of the books, just in case something interesting to me had somehow crept in there, but all I could see was row upon row of unadulterated dullness. If there were such things as haunted books, I thought, tracts on engineering and the dutiful produce of the Society for the Promotion of Christian Knowledge were surely the least vulnerable of all imaginable texts to such a curse.

"Are you're sure it's the stock that's the cause of the…problem?" I asked him. "Hauntings are traditionally associated with locations rather than the objects in them—usually with nasty events of some kind."

Lionel could probably have intervened with a dozen contradictory anecdotes, and Penny might well have had an entire dossier of SPR research to quote, but they were still unpacking equipment from cases, so Martin's embarrassment was able to increase without the immediate possibility of relief.

"I'm sure there's no connection with…the other thing," he said, hurriedly.

"What other thing?" I asked, unable to pick up the cryptic reference.

"Fred West," he mumbled.

It was then only then that I remembered the serial killer's ashes had been scattered on Barry Island a couple of years earlier, following his suicide. It occurred to me that if Martin's wife had fond memories of the resort, she might have thought that a trifle sinister. If she was now refusing to step into the shop, it might be because s   he was thinking more in terms of Nightmare on Elm Street than luckmen's grimoires, and that Martin's determination to put the blame on the books might have a certain defensive logic to it.

"Right," I said, figuring that the kindest thing to do was at least try to help him out with that. "Do you have any suspicion as to which particular books might be involved?"

"Not really," he said—but I noticed that his eyes reflectively looked up toward the first floor: the section where he'd put the fiction, and other material he thought not worth distributing in his principal display space. It occurred to me then that he hadn't offered to show me, or Penny round the premises, and I couldn't help wondering because he was reluctant, if only unconsciously, to go upstairs.

Penny was still busy setting up her apparatus, including thermometers, voice recorders and other measuring devices, presumably more sophisticated than those with which Harry Price had fitted out his famous laboratory, but Lionel was unoccupied again, seemingly giving full attention to the conversation. He had obviously noticed Martin's glance because he too looked up at the ceiling, speculatively—but he didn't immediately head for the stairs.

"You didn't pick up the libraries from any haunted pits, then," I suggested to Martin, thinking of it as a joke, but also thinking that if his wife was subtly haunted by the notion that Fred West's evil spirit might have been transported to Barry with his ashes, Martin, as a career mining man, might have older narratives at the back of his mind: narratives that he had never permitted himself to believe, for professional as well as philosophical reasons, but still retained in the darker depths of his consciousness.

"Well," he said, a trifle sheepishly, "I did pick up a couple of hundred from the old Glofeydd Diafol." While married to the Ex I had managed to pick up a very slight smattering of Welsh terminology, and had been struck by her assurance that, much as Eskimos are reputed to have a dozen different words for snow, the southern Welsh have at least eight different terms for coalmine. I guessed readily enough that glofeydd was probably one of them, and it didn't take a genius to work out what diafol meant.

"It's just a nickname, like," Martin added. "Its name on the maps is Pwllmerys. Old mine, not very big, remote—but unusual."

"Unusual how?" asked Lionel, who was all ears now. He was from Norfolk originally, but he knew as well as I did, given his professional interest, that *diafol* meant "devil."

Martin, of course, had a mining engineer's notion of *unusual*. "You probably think all coal is the same," he said, "but you'd be wrong, partly because of the different degrees of metamorphosis, which determine the carbon content, and partly because of variations in the impurities mingled with the carbon in the coarser varieties—sulfur and the like. Even high-grade coal—anthracite, that is—which is more than 92% carbon, can vary quite significantly in the composition of the remaining few per cent, especially in terms of complex organic molecules that haven't been broken down completely. Anthracite is typically very hard, but it's not necessarily the case that all coal with a high carbon content is rocky, and there are some anomalous seams that are surprisingly soft even though they're 95% carbon, and relatively deep-lying. Pwyllmerys is one of those. In terms of its carbon content it's akin to high-grade anthracite, but it's uncommonly friable, which means that it produces a hell of a lot of dust when it's hewn.

"Pwyllmerys used to be notorious in the valleys as the filthiest pit in Wales, an' the villagers were foisted, perhaps unkindly, with the reputation of being the filthiest people. It wasn't helped by the fact that the shacks that grew up around the pithead as the enterprise became industrialized never became a proper village, because they never built a chapel. That and the dust earned the pit the nickname of Glofeydd Diafol ...and once they had it, naturally, stories were made up about the pitmen being visited by and on friendly terms with the Devil...and maybe some of them began to believe it themselves. Not difficult to see things when you're working a seam in the dark, believe me, with the dangers of collapse, flooding and firedamp everpresent."

"And you got the remnants of the old pithead library?" I said.

"Someone up there heard I was shopping around," Marrtin said, defensively. "He rang me up and offered it. Said no one in the village was interested any more but that in the old days, the pitmen had been as proud as anyone else of their work, and as keen as anyone to improve their minds— resentful, I guess, of way the anthracite miners regarded them. Precisely because it was reputed to be the shittiest pit in Wales, stuck up the arse end of nowhere, some weird educational organization made it a point to donate them a library of sorts, way back in the 1840s, although I can't imagine that any books from that period actually survived into the twentieth century."

Lionel and I had both pricked up our eras at that news. "What was *weird* about it?" Lionel demanded.

"Not supernatural weird," Martin was quick to say. "French."

That increased my interest rather than diminishing it. "You mean the *Societé des Connaissances Utiles?*" I asked "Émile de Girardin's organization, of one of its branches?"

Martin shrugged his shoulders, never having heard of Émile de Girardin. "The books they supplied weren't French, of course," he added. "Probably acquired locally."

At any rate, I thought, they were perhaps more likely to be in English than in Welsh, and, more to the point, the members of the Societé in question, being closely associated with the French Romantic Movement, were likely to have a much broader notion of what constituted useful knowledge and uplifting reading material than the S.P.C.K.

"And those books are upstairs, right?" I said.

"In the alcove by the window," Martin confirmed, "but I should never have taken them up there, or even accepted them in the first place, no matter how reluctant I was to have made such a long trip for nothing...."

"Because you think they're the haunted ones?" Lionel hypothesized, looking upwards again.

"God, no," Martin retorted. "Because they're absolutely bloody filthy. Like I said, I can't imagine than any go back to the early nineteenth century, but I can't say I've examined them closely, because you can't open them up without releasing a cloud of fine black dust. It was okay while they were still in the boxes, but as soon as I started transferring them to shelves—even as far as I got, which wasn't far—the dust started coming out, and I realized that it had been a really bad idea even to accept them as a gift."

He looked at me with a slightly critical eye, obviously taking note of the fact that I was, as always, dressed completely in black, whereas he was wearing a pale gray jacket and a gleaming white shirt. Lionel's clothing was also dark, but I noticed Penny looking down at her own tasteful outfit, evidently having belated second thoughts about the wisdom of carrying out a ghost-watch in a shop full of relics of the mining industry.

"You might not show it like I did," Martin opined, addressing me, "but believe me, if you're actually thinking of taking the rest out of the boxes an' looking at the damn things one by one, your jacket will have to go to the dry cleaners an' you'll be giving off a miasma until you can put everything else you're wearing through the washing machine. My advice is to leave them alone. I'll come back in my overalls before I open the shop, stick them all in sacks to go on the fire, an' go over the upper room three times over with a good vac."

The horror was probably legible on my face. "You can't put them on the fire," I said, "at least until they've been properly checked over, to make sure that there's nothing interesting among them, however dusty it might be."

"Well, good luck with that," he said, "but try to keep them at arm's length, and don't come near me when you come back downstairs again. Supernatural presences might set the nerves on edge, but dirt is just muck—and you can't exorcize muck."

I thought about that for a moment or two. It was getting late but it was still light and still mild, even though the sky was overcast. I took my jacket off, and then, after testing the air temperature, took my T-shirt off too. I remembered what Martin had said about the bathroom facilities being primitive but he had mentioned a sink, and had presumably laid in soap and towels. There was a roll of bubble-wrap behind the counter, presumably in optimistic items of parceling up any books ordered by mail; I tore off a generous strip and wrapped it around my waist and thighs like a sarong.

Penny, in particular, looked at me as if I had gone completely mad. Bare-chested, I certainly do not have the physique of a body-builder, but needs must, as they day, when the devil drives, and if I was going to have to tussle with the world's worst coal-dust in order to get a look inside the books from Glofeydd Diafol, I figured that the least I could do was not mind too much about looking ridiculous while I did so.

"If he really is going to sort through those boxes," Martin said to Penny and Lionel, "you might want to take a quick look upstairs now, and then leave him to it."

Only Lionel accepted the invitation, and went immediately up to sample the supernatural atmosphere. Penny checked with Martin, who assured her that the "presence" was evident all over the shop, and decided to avoid the top room for the time being.

"Don't worry," I assured her. "I'll leave the corner in question until last and check the other shelves first, so there'll still be plenty of time for you to take a look around up there if you want to."

"Very kind of you," I'm sure, said Penny, giving the impression that she had no immediate plans to take advantage of the concession. It was interesting to observe the inroads that a peach blouse and gray skirt could make into the boldness of the hardiest ghost-hunter, especially one who didn't feel that she had the option, as I had, of stripping to the waist.

"It's okay," I said, casting a significant successive glance over Martin's white shirt, Penny's blouse and Lionel' clerical collar, once the last-named had returned from his rapid inspection of the first floor, "I'll find my own way around up there. I might be gone some time, but I dare say that the dust will have settled before you get round to thinking about sending out a search party."

CHAPTER IV

Before the ascent I cast a critical eye over the rickety staircase that led up to the first floor, carpeted in what had once been red felt but had probably been almost completely black even before Martin had carried the boxes full of the remnants of the Glofeydd Diafol library upstairs. "Where's the switch for the upstairs lights?" I asked Martin, for future reference.

"There's one at the top on the left," he informed me, "and another just inside the door of the front room. You shouldn't need them yet, though— the windows up there let in more light than this one."

As I headed up the stairs I could feel renewed optimism putting a spring in my step. The uncluttered window of the short corridor and the one visible through the open door of the bathroom did indeed let in more light than the window downstairs whose exposure was masked by the houses on the other side of the street, but they were also smaller, so the advantage was not as marked as I could have wished. Even so, I left the electric switch alone as I stepped through the open door into the room directly over the shop-front.

As soon as I had moved into the room the feeling hit me. It took me completely by surprise, and the impact was sufficient to make me catch my breath.

I had been in that room before.

It was at that moment, I think, that my odyssey in the surreal really began. From that first step into the upper room, albeit with a relatively slow start, things got curiouser and curiouser.

I had, of course, experienced the commonplace sensation of *déjà-vu* before, but never so intensely as to make me doubt the conventional explanation that it arises from an illusion generated when the same sensory information is accidentally duplicated in the brain, having been transmitted there by two distinct neuronal pathways. This was different, not just because of its intensity but because I knew—vaguely, at least—when and where I had had the experience that was being so carefully and so improbably reproduced by the present moment.

Most people, it is said, have recurring dreams. They may dream repeatedly of houses, of sexual encounters, of flying, or of appearing naked in public. When they have such dreams—or, at least, when they become conscious that they're having such dreams—they know that they're revisiting scenes already familiar: that the house they're in is one they have previously visited in dreams, or that their power of flight is something that they are *re*discovering. Some such dreams may be enigmatic, perhaps because they're symbolically-disguised, but others are trivially literal; mine have always been perfectly understandable. My own recurrent dreams, in those days, were almost always of second-hand bookshops.

I had never considered it at all unusual that my long-standing addiction to combing the shelves of second-hand bookshops should be reflected in my dreams. Nor had I ever considered it unusual that such dreams should often be attended by the sense of returning to familiar haunts—because that, after all, is the form that the vast majority of my actual book-hunting trips took. It was only to be expected, in 1997, that when I dreamed about bookshops—or, at least, when I became conscious that I was dreaming about a bookshops—I usually felt that they were familiar bookshops. Interestingly, however, they never seemed to be bookshops that really do exist in the everyday world; they were always imaginary bookshops. That meant, of course, that when I had the sense of having visited them before, I knew that I could only have done so in other dreams. It was as if the virtual geography of my private dream-world numbered among its fixtures a series of shops, some fascinating and some not-so-fascinating, which I visited at irregular intervals: a population parallel to that with which the geography of the real world was dotted.

I use the past tense, of course, not merely because I no longer visit second-hand bookshops and no longer dream about them, but because the world has changed decisively in the interim, second-hand bookshops having virtually disappeared from England under the double hit of the uniform business rate and the spread of Oxfam bookshops, whose operators do not have to pay for their stock.

Sometimes, when dreaming about bookshops in the old days, I became conscious that I was dreaming—but I always resisted waking up, because I knew that when I did I would have to leave behind any interesting books I might have found. When my bookshop dreams became lucid in that fashion I often became conscious of the fact—or at least the illusion—that the shop I was in was one of which I had dreamed before.

Just as I had never dreamed about entering a bookshop that actually existed, so I had never previously entered an actual bookshop about which I had dreamed. That I seemed to be doing so at that particular moment was, therefore, more than a cause for astonishment; it seemed, in fact, almost to be a violation of natural law, as threatening in its fashion as any conventional apparition or ominous shadow. I stood transfixed, appalled by the thought that I—a supposedly great and hitherto worthy champion of skepticism—could be assailed in that rude and nasty fashion.

Mercifully, the moment didn't last. The shock of awful discovery was replaced soon enough by a struggle to remember what, if anything, I had found in the room when it had only been the figment of a dream. The mental reflex of the book-collector was powerful enough to drive away the alarm of revelation; I ceased to worry about the *how* of the mystery and focused my mind instead on the truly crucial question of what there might be to be found, and whether the illusion of having dreamed about the room—I was already content to dismiss the sensation as an illusion—might somehow assist my search.

As I had promised, I did not begin with the alcove by the window, whose shelves were almost bare, only containing, at present, fewer than thirty aligned books, although half a dozen more-or-less densely-packed cardboard boxes were still piled up in front of them. It seemed far more sensible to start by examining the safer stock, coal-dust-wise.

No sooner had I begun to scan the nearest shelves, however, than the force of reality began to reassert itself upon my senses. The proportion of Welsh texts here was considerably less than on the shelves below—considerably less than half, although not entirely negligible—but that didn't make the remainder seem significantly more promising. There were several sets of standard authors, more poetry than prose, in horribly shabby pocket editions. My expert eye immediately picked out a number of yellowbacks, but their condition was so awful that it would hardly have mattered had they been more interesting titles than they were. A few bound volumes of old periodicals turned out on closer inspection to be *Sunday at Home* and *Pick-Me-Up*, not even *Longman's* or *Temple Bar*, let alone anything more interesting.

In brief, it looked like the kind of stock over which a collector might toil for hours in order to turn up a couple of items whose significance to his collection was marginal at best. Not, of course, that I could contentedly let it alone; I knew that I would indeed have to inspect every single shelf, lifting every volume whose title was not clearly inscribed on its spine, in order to make perfectly certain that nothing evaded me. No matter how laborious the task became, I thought I would have to stick to it come hell or high water—but I had only been at it for half an hour when I was summoned to return downstairs, in answer to Lionel's urgent call.

Assuming that he or one of his companions had felt something eerie, even though the sun had only just set and the twilight had not faded, or that Penny's measuring devices had picked up a sharp drop in temperature or some kind of mysterious atmospheric ionization, I hastened down the hazardous stairs—but it turned out to be a false alarm.

All that Lionel wanted, it turned out, was to hand me a cup of tea and ask my opinion as to what kind of pizza he ought to have delivered.

There is nothing like a four-way debate about pizza toppings to bring a ghost-hunting expedition right down to earth; by the time we had settled on two mediums, one with bacon, mushroom and tomato and the other with olives, anchovies and pepperoni, mundanity had such a secure hold on Martin's bookshop, even with the electric lights now on, that Madame Arcati at her most lunatic would have been hard-pressed to find the least hint of spirit activity.

All the SPR's apparatus was lying idle. The video camera was on its tripod, ready to be spun around in quest of the kinds of things that one glimpses in the corners of one's eyes, and a quaint little pointer was ready to inscribe a record of the room's temperature on a slowly-rotating drum, but they were inactive. Although I still wasn't sure what the ammeter was hooked up to, whatever it was had not yet succeeded in generating a flicker of current. All of it gave the impression of having already given up rather than being eager to begin.

I was glad to note, however, having consulted one of the thermometers, that since we had entered the shop our combined body-heat had contrived to raise the temperature by a whole degree Celsius to sixteen, perfectly comfortable even with my shirt off.

Lionel asked Penny to tell him a little more about luckmen and their role in the mines of yore, but Penny had already run to the limit of her information on the subject. As I confessed that I had not yet touched the legacy of Glofeydd Diafol, that topic lay fallow too, at least in the specific sense. Penny did endeavor to pump Martin about residual superstitions in the modern industry in general—apparently thinking more as a sociologist than a paranormal researcher—but it was a subject on which he was not particularly forthcoming.

"I was always above ground, see," he said. "The boys at the face had their own little community—they'd tell you tales for a laugh, like, but they'd never let on that they took any of it seriously."

"What kind of tales?" Penny wanted to know. Lionel was obviously interested too, and I was always ready to hear anything that I could appropriate for use in a story.

"*You* know," said Martin, although we really didn't. "Not a pit in the valley has a clean sheet mortality-wise—not any that's still working has been open much longer than twenty years. Even so, the oldest ones are full of worked-out shafts and old rock falls, an' there's always talk of voices— voices of men killed by gas or crushed, you see. Offering warnings as often as not; I've heard far more tales of men being saved than men being lost. Nobody goes down a pit needs scaring, see; work's dangerous enough without that."

"Judging by the dust on some of the books upstairs, even those that didn't come from the Devil's pit," I said, "one or two of them must have made a good number of trips down into the shafts."

"I doubt that," Martin said. "No time to read down there, nor any light good enough to read by. The dust on the bindings even of the books from the hard anthracite pits is the kind that gets in everywhere—the fine stuff that hangs about in the air and never quite washes out. Almost like a liquid, it is—a *miasma*, as I said before—tends to smear and cling and blacken even if you never set foot in the cage or put a hand on a hopper. You can imagine how much worse it is when it comes from soft stuff like the coal from Pwllmerys."

I had to admire the way he pronounced "miasma", lingering over the vowels as only a Welshman could.

"The dark spirit of the pit," said Penny, softly. It would almost have been enough to make us look over our shoulders if we hadn't heard the delivery boy's moped rattling over the potholes in the street. We fell upon the pizza-slices with the kind of eager rapacity that only competition can generate, even though we all knew perfectly well that we were only entitled to four apiece.

While we ate, darkness fell—and shadows crept upon us in spite of the electric light. Martin, born and bred to the economy of the valleys, had only fitted sixty-watt bulbs.

Martin was watching us now, alert for any sign of tension or unease. As with many Celts, his eyes were pale even though his hair was dark, but they weren't blue; they were as grey as slate. Although Penny was a very different physical type—ectomorphic rather than endomorphic—she had very similar coloring. Her eyes did retain a slight hint of blue but her complexion lacked the hint of rosy pink that Martin's had. Lionel must have been at least twenty years older than Martin and thirty years older than Penny but he looked more robust than either of them. Being from a long line of East Anglians didn't necessarily make him an Angle by ancestry; like me, he could just as easily be a descendant of Viking settlers. At any rate, *our* ancestors had never been bards or druids; our family trees were as devoid of luckmen as of mistletoe.

I was prepared to feel a slight pang of regret about that; I knew that if I were going to find any real treasure in that dust-caked morass upstairs I was going to need some luck. Even while we ate, my restless eyes were checking and rechecking the downstairs shelves, unable to find anything worth lingering over.

The pizza was as mediocre as could be expected, but the tea was bet-ter. It seemed much better until I got to the dregs, when I began to notice an odd aftertaste. I noticed, too, that the air in the shop had a peculiar texture to it.

All bookshops are dusty, of course, and when books that have been a long time in storage are first set on shelves they often release a little dampness into the air, faintly polluted with fungal spores and bits of dead silverfish. Book-lovers learn to savor that kind of atmosphere, or at least to ignore it—but this texture was slightly different from any I'd encountered before. It gave the impression of being vintage dust—a real *grand cru*. Martin's pronunciation of the word "miasma" echoed in my mind as I tried to measure the dust's quality more precisely, but it didn't seem dismissable simply as coal-dust any more than it warranted elevation to the status of "the dark spirit of the pit". It was something more teasing than either.

I couldn't help thinking of the skeptical kind of occult detective stories, where the intrepid investigators eventually find that alleged hauntings are merely noxious vapors released from bad drains or unusual chemical reactions. Was it possible, I wondered, that the redistribution of books kept so long in close confinement really had set free some disturbing vapor that had been patiently building up in the inner recesses of the boxes for decades?

Perhaps it wasn't impossible, I thought, that even the coal dust might contain some exotic organic compound among the pollutants that still remained alongside the pure metamorphosed carbon. Coal was, after all, the ultimate residue of dead plant matter, which presumably included not merely giant ferns, horsetails and cycads, but all manner of fungi. What sort of coal, I wondered, might magic mushrooms make after a few tens of millions of years of patient squeezing?

But then, there was also the other component of dust that I'd mentioned in *Chacun sa goule*. Recent household dust is mostly the residue of human skin, and that skin has been compounded while alive out of the residues of older carbonaceous matter, because there are fragments of past lives in the very air we breathe...lives that had once been mindful, inhabited by the stuff of dreams and souls. If, as had been suggested by some physicists, subatomic particles once paired retain a strange kind of association even when separated, the particles making up our bodies might still be in arcane contact with the fugitive substance of all manner of past lives, all manner of ghostly echoes....

On the other hand, as Martin said, maybe whatever was causing the tea's funny aftertaste was just unromanticized "muck." And it might be worth remembering, too, I thought at the time, that coalmines produce methane as well as coal.

I didn't like to suggest to the others that perhaps we should have brought a canary.

"Well," I said, as soon as I had bolted my last allotted slice of bacon, mushroom and tomato. "I'm going to get back to the upstairs stock—hundreds of volumes to go even before I get to the sinister corner where the darkest spirit of all is lurking. If you need me, just scream."

"Will you be all right up there on your own now that it's dark?" Martin asked, as if he sincerely believed that I might not be, even with the support of electric light.

"If I'm not," I assured him, "*I'll* scream."

"If you find any of mine," said Lionel, "let me know." Long before he got religion Lionel was the most prolific writer of science fiction and supernatural fiction in Britain, producing over a hundred and eighty volumes for the late unlamented Badger Books for the princely fee of £22 10s a time. His one long-running series had consisted of occult detective stories starring the redoubtable Val Stearman and his lovely female associate La Noire. Stearman had, of course, been modeled on the young Lionel, and his spirit was doubtless still active even though the containing flesh had suffered a little. It would have required an extremely optimistic eye, alas, to find the slightest hint of La Noire in Penny-from-the-SPR at that moment in time.

"I will," I promised.

CHAPTER V

The electric lights turned out to be less bright than I could have hoped. I made a mental note to bring my own hundred-watt bulbs if I ever got involved in a similar vigil in future. I had started my search in the top left-hand corner of the shelf-unit to the left of the door and had begun to work methodically across and down, across and down. I had completed approximately half of one wall, and I had no difficulty in finding the exact spot where I'd left off.

If you've ever browsed the less popular shelves in the London Library, as I often did in those days and still do on occasion, you'll know how dust from red leather bindings that are gradually rotting down will stain your hands and your shirt, so that a long session in French Fiction can leave you looking suspiciously like Jack the Ripper, or Fred West on a busy day. Exploring those shelves was not dissimilar, although any red dye in the older bindings had been blackened long ago—and I was still exploring the books that had come from the more respectable pits. I began to feel very glad that the awful warnings abut the legacy of Glofeydd Diafol had caused me to take precautions in my mode of undress, although I soon began to look down at my arms and chest with definite pangs of regret regarding the absence of a shower from the shop's bathroom. I had noticed a flannel dangling over the edge of the sink, but I figured that I was going to have to make abundant use of it, and I was beginning to suspect that my face might have begun to look like the flank of a blurred zebra.

I tried to look on the bright side, reminding myself that my corduroy jacket and T-short were safely downstairs and that my jeans were at least partly-protected by the bubble-wrap. I also told myself that at least it couldn't get any worse when I finally got to the corner I was saving for last. I thought that at the time because, as Martin had suggested, even the dust from the vicinity of the more orthodox pits was so fine as to be *slick* and it soon made itself evident in its texture as well as color. If the dust had been pure carbon it might, I suppose, have been reminiscent of graphite, but even the dust of the best Welsh anthracite was still sufficiently impure to enhance its ability to form a miasma.

I couldn't help wiping my hands periodically on the bubble-wrap, even though I knew that it wasn't helping the situation. Nor could I help occasionally touching my hand to my face, my forehead and my hair, even though I knew that such touches would make the smudges worse. By the time I'd done a further thirty feet of shelves—without finding a single book that I'd have been happy to pay more than 50p for—I knew that I must be a real sight, and what Martin had said in the car about the woeful inadequacy of the bathroom facilities suddenly began to seem like a prophetic cry of woe.

Despite the aforementioned inadequacy, my companions stumped up the staircase one by one to use the facilities. Lionel was the only one who took the risk of looking into the front room to see how I was doing, and he hardly stepped across the threshold, although he had no reason at all to fear supernatural presences, being a fully-armed exorcist. When I stopped for a break myself I took the opportunity to inspect my features in the mirror, and I managed to scrub off the worst of the stains with toilet paper, but even a thorough soaping failed to shift the worst of the grime from my fingers.

As I resumed my labors I remembered yet again what I'd written in "*Chacun sa goule*" about our breathing in the carbon dioxide relics of the dead every time we fill our lungs, and this time I thought about the lives and deaths of the men who had hewed the coal, and that minority among them who had tried, valiantly, to improve their minds with the aid of the written word, poring over the pages I was now turning, probably ashamed of the residual dust on their fingers that no amount of washing had been able to remove.

Once, at the University of Reading, I had attended an open lecture give by A. N. Wilson, shortly after having completed his life of Jesus, in which he had argued that the rich inner life of thought and feeling, which we now take completely for granted, is largely a product of books, and most especially of novels. Men who lived and died confined by oral culture, Wilson had argued, had not the mental resources to build a robust inner monologue, a pressurized stream of consciousness. I hadn't believed him at the time, but I thought while I was standing in Martin's bookshop that if it *had* been true, such men could hardly be in any position to leave ghosts behind when they died and decayed. If dust really could retain some kind of spirit, it would, of necessity, be the spirit of *readers*—in which case, book-dust ought to be the most enspirited of all.

As I formed that strange thought, the sensation of having been in that room before returned in full force, swiftly and irresistibly.

I didn't pause in my routine of plucking the books off the shelves, inspecting their title-pages and returning them, but the automatism of that routine suddenly became oppressive and seemingly unnatural. Before, when the sensation had come over me, I had thought it an anomaly: a sensation that I should only have been capable of feeling in a dream—but now it didn't feel anomalous at all, because it seemed now that I really was *in a dream*, where I was perfectly entitled to remember bookshops visited in other dreams, and to dwell in the curious nostalgia of discoveries barely made before that had been lost in previous moments of awakening.

As in all such episodes of lucidity, I had not the slightest desire to wake up; indeed, I had the strongest possible desire to remain as I was, potentially able to grasp and hold any treasure that wishful thinking might deliver into my horridly pitch-black hand.

The light of the sixty-watt bulb seemed to grow dimmer, and the walls of the room seemed to draw closer. The spines of the books seemed to grow darker, and the air seemed to become thicker and heavier. Because I knew, or imagined, that I was in a dream-state, I wasn't unduly worried—on the contrary, I was intent on preserving a state in which the power of desire might be adequate to lead me to a precious find. It occurred to me that the room had become uncannily like a pit, both literally and metaphorically. The dross on the shelves was the mere stone matrix of the imagination, inert and useless, while the texts for which I was searching were pregnant with mental energy that only needed to be read in order to warm and il-luminate my inner being.

Because my collection already possessed twenty thousand volumes in 1997, my want list had been shrinking for years, and the works that I yearned most desperately to find at that time were so rare that it would have require a veritable miracle of luck to locate affordable copies. Without any magical ritual to aid me in my search through Martin's stock I had only honest toil to bring to my task: a simple, straightforward determina-tion to make certain that nothing would escape my notice. I searched with relentless efficiency. I worked methodically along the shelves, ignoring the miasmic dust, in the frail hope that somewhere beneath its obscuring cloak a treasure trove might be waiting: a copy of *Gyphantia*, or *Omegarus and Syderia*, or *The Mummy!*, or *The Old Maid's Talisman*, in any edition and any condition, provided only that the text was complete.

It eventually became so difficult to draw breath that I felt slightly dizzy, and it seemed to have become so dark that I had no alternative but to pause in my work. By then I had found a handful of books that I actu-ally wanted to acquire, although there was nothing particularly valuable. I laid them carefully on the floor, in the cleanest corner of the room before I moved in to the final phase of my search: the alcove by the window.

The lighting in the covert was peculiar, because of the combination of the shadow of the corner of the alcove, which blocked some of the light from the sixty-watt bulb, and the light of a street-lamp coming in obliquely through the window. The sum of the two effects would have provided enough light to read titles on spines had any titles still been visible, but none were. Although I had thought that matters had got so bad, dust-wise, that there was not much margin for getting worse, I had been seriously mistaken. The books from Glofeydd Diafol were an order of magnitude worse than those from the other pits and Workingmen's Institutes. Black is black, you might think, and so it is, but there are nevertheless intensities in blackness, and, as I had already found out, there was the question of texture to be taken into account, and the potential not merely for thickening the surrounding atmosphere but transforming it, into a miasma that was not merely steeped in shadow, but a particular species of shadow.

Resolutely, I inspected the books that Martin had already set out on the shelves, and then I began on the boxes, methodically completing the work of shelving that Martin had begun, inspecting the title-page of each volume before lining it up neatly, in a file that soon filled the upper shelves and moved steadily downwards.

They were, alas, the most boring books imaginable. The hopes raised by the involvement to Émile de Girardin's society or one of it branches were soon dashed. Thirty per cent of the books were Welsh, and thirty per cent of those in English were familiar religious tracts. The volumes of philosophy and history were all cheap reprints of commonplace texts, and the poetry and fiction consisted of broken sets of standard authors. Nevertheless, I kept going.

If you're going to be obsessed, you have to take it seriously. If you start a search, you have to finish it, and you have to take what comfort you can from the fact that there really will come a time, eventually, where your skin really can't absorb any more coal-dust, even of the softest and silkiest kind imaginable.

By the time I began to feel ill I was already kneeling down, inspecting the lowest shelves in the unit, so I was in no danger of falling over, but I had to put out a hand nevertheless to support myself against the shelves. My eyes had begun to play tricks on me; phosphenes lit up the black air like a cluster of stars, and the darkness itself had begun to flow and shift, as if it were alive with a host of bustling shades like the ones that must have clustered around Orpheus in the Underworld, eager to hear his nourishing music: a host so vast and so crowded that its individual parts seemed to jostling for presence in a narrow corridor that was growing narrower and more suffocating by the instant.

The dust that saturated the atmosphere around my head now seemed so dense that the air gave the impression of being liquid rather than gaseous. My trachea had closed reflexively, and I found myself gulping, swallowing the air and the intoxicating spirit that possessed and saturated it. It seemed to be seeping into my being through my gut, my lungs and my every pore, reaching for my heart.

I told myself sternly, however, that it was all illusion, that I'd just got slightly carried away in my search for printed arcana, and that any symptoms I felt were merely psychotropic.

It's just muck, I told myself. *All I need is a wash. Ten minutes with the flannel, and I'll be fine.*

I wasn't afraid. I was strangely secure in my lurking conviction that an instant of effort would be enough to bring me out of the apparent dream-state and back to wakefulness, whenever I wanted to emerge, and I had dreamed far too many dreams of that frail kind to allow panic any moment of opportunity. So I drank the spirits of the dead in dream-like fashion, and drank them gladly. I even drank them thirstily, because I knew that they were closer to me than any mere kin. What was my own spirit, after all, but a compound of all that I had read and inwardly digested?

Even if A. N. Wilson had been as direly mistaken in his estimate of the majority of men as I suspected, I thought, he was surely right about himself and he was right about me. *My* inner life, *my* pressurized stream of consciousness, was the product of texts and the love of texts. I had been a ghoul all my life; of what had I to be afraid, in that dark room full of clamorous spirits? The greater part of my life, and the greater part of my emotion, had been spent and generated by intercourse with the dead; what need had I to feel threatened, or even to suspect the presence of maleficent evil, in the dust of books?

Except, of course, that it wasn't, strictly speaking, the dust of books: it was coal-dust, the residue of life far older than any thinking life…or at least, any thinking life of which we are aware, or capable of envisaging.

At any rate, I seemed, in my dream-like state of consciousness, to be drinking deeply, avid for further intoxication. And why not? The dust was, after all, a previously-untasted vintage.

I felt slightly stirred, as if a moist wind and a cloying warmth were washing over me but leaving no impression. I felt as if the fading ruddy gleams of the Celtic twilight were in my lungs and in my heart. I felt as if the heritage of Merlin and Taliesin, and the force of Druid magic, were in my brain and in my groin. I thought I could hear the musical voices of luckmen intoning their spells, mingled with the strangled cries of hewers of coal choked by firedamp or crushed by falling stone, all echoing together in the empty spaces of my mind.

It was a strangely delicious fantasy, a poignantly haunting dream: a fantasy so delicious and a dream so haunting that there was a moment when I would dearly have liked to maintain it against the cruel penetration of lucidity—but it is exactly that moment of yearning, in a real dream, that precipitates the return of normal consciousness. Because I became all too conscious that I was dreaming, I could not maintain the altered state of mind. My innate skepticism reminded me that, at the end of the day, the black stuff that I had released while descending the shelves was really just muck.

My supporting hand moved along the wooden shelf and my senses reeled. It was only the slightest of adjustments but my little finger picked a thin splinter out of the distressed wood, and the tiny stab of pain made me gasp. The gasp turned to a cough, and then to a fit of coughing—and a cataract of black dust cascaded out of my open mouth into the palm of my hand.

The sixty-watt bulb buzzed and flickered, and its light became noticeably brighter. I hauled myself to my feet, blinked away the moment of narcotic drowsiness, breathed in cleaner and cooler air, pulled myself together, and then went directly to the bathroom in order to rinse my hands before picking up the flannel and starting the serious business of cleaning myself up.

At first, when I looked in the mirror, my face was reminiscent of an infernal imp, but that impression could not prevail, in the fullness of time, against the pressure of soap and hot water. Methodically, I cleaned myself up, washing away the sin of obsessive book-lust, the cardinal vice of the Faustian Age.

I didn't curse myself for having lost my grip on the dream-state. Once full consciousness had reasserted itself, ir easily regained its privileges and its hegemony. Dreams are by nature fragile and fugitive, and only death can free us, in the end, from the everpresent duty of waking from their toils. Until then, I told myself, as the flannel did its work, it is probably best to put their temporary hauntings away in the coverts of forgetfulness, and be glad.

Always assuming of course, that you can.

CHAPTER VI

In the short term, that didn't seem to be a problem. The careful washing of my face, hair, chest and arms not only freed me of almost all the dust that had stuck to me externally, but also seemed to scrub away any vestiges of malaise or hallucination. I had a slight aftertaste in my mouth, understandably, and when I blew my nose the handkerchief developed an ugly black stain, but I didn't go into full-blown allergic rhinitis. By the time I was ready to go back downstairs I felt as steady as a rock.

Eventually, I made my way back to my fellow investigators, clutching my meager booty. The best items I had found were a couple of bound volumes of *Reynolds' Miscellany*, including the serial version of G. W. M. Reynolds' *Faust*, and battered copies of Eugène Sue's *Martin the Foundling*, George Griffith's *A Criminal Croesus*, and Mrs. Riddell's *Fairy Water*. They were all in mediocre condition, but they were all titles that I'd be glad to add to my collection. Considering that the hunt had started and finished so unpromisingly it didn't seem to be a bad haul, and there was still a slight possibility that I could add to it from the ground floor stock.

Lionel, Martin, and Penny were sitting downstairs, as quiet as church mice. I thought at first that they might be asleep, even though the light was on, and I took care to tiptoe down the last few steps, but Lionel looked around as I reached the floor and said: "There's more tea in the pot. We've all had a second cup." His voice was slower than usual and a little thicker.

"I'm okay," I assured him. "Seen any sign of *the presence*?"

"Not *seen*, exactly," he told me, "but we've definitely felt something, haven't we?"

"It's not as bad as it has been," Martin said, perhaps slightly disgruntled by the failure of his shop to come up with the supernatural goods, "but I can definitely feel it."

"How about you?" I said to Penny.

"There doesn't seem to be anything objective," she said, looking sadly at her various instruments. "But I can certainly feel *something*. It's faint, but it's there." I could tell from the tone of her voice that she was disappointed. It's hard to impress people with subjective feelings; she knew that unless she could carry away some kind of tangible record—a clip of film, a trace on her rotating chart or a leaping needle on the ammeter—she'd have nothing to interest the punctilious inquisitors of the Society for Psychical Research.

"Is there anything upstairs?" Lionel asked, obviously expecting a negative answer, probably because it was me that he was asking rather than a suspicion that whatever was causing his uneasy feeling was limited to the ground floor.

"Just books," I said, instinctively protecting my reputation for skepticism as well as being what I thought was honest. "Hundreds and hundreds that no one will ever want to read—and a few dozen that someone might. I've only found a few, but they won't just sit on my shelves unread. I feel sorry for the rest, in a way. All the thought that went into their creation! All the mental effort! If they only had voices, they'd be clamoring for attention, don't you think? They'd be excited, wouldn't they, at having been taken out of their coffins at last and put on display? The ones from Glofeydd Diafol—which I finished shelving for you, by the way, Martin, albeit not in alphabetical or subject order—will be particularly glad to see the light of day again when dawn breaks, after so long stewing in the dark, in their own miasma."

Martin didn't thank me for that effort; I guessed that he hadn't changed his mind about intending to clear out all the dirtiest items from the upstairs room and storing them in the coal-hole for use as winter fuel when the season changed. Having inspected them, that thought no longer seemed quite as horribly sacrilegious to me as it had before.

In fact, I mused—but didn't vocalize—the books in question might well have thought, had they been capable of thinking, that the Day of Judgment had come when Martin had first unpacked them. Perhaps some of the more optimistic had thought that, at least in a just world, they might be bound for paradise rather than the inferno, but disillusionment must be setting in, now that I had passed them before my censorious eye and found them wanting.

How long, I wondered, would it take a book to give way to despair? Not long, I expected, if it were a book from a colliery library—a book that had already had a taste of the darkness of the abyss in the eyes and mind of its readers.

"You're not taking this seriously, are you, Mr. Stableford?" Martin observed, without undue rancor. "It's all just a joke to you."

"Well," I said, "I'm truly sorry if you think that my skeptical presence is somehow inhibiting the paranormal manifestations. I honesty would prefer it if the night turned out to be exciting—even alarming. On the other hand you might have cause to be grateful if skepticism causes the phenomenon to evaporate without even waiting to be exorcized."

Lionel nodded sympathetically, evidently still feeling that exorcism ought to be reckoned a latest report. Martin, however, seemed to have had enough, and just wanted to get the night over with, whatever the result and its consequences might turn out to be.

"The trouble with skeptics," Penny added, taking care to couch her remarks in general terms, "is that they're too enthusiastic to accept their own insensitivity as proof that there's nothing to be sensitive to. They're like blind men denying that sight is possible. Not everyone's the same, you know. Everybody's different, and some people can feel the presence of things that others can't."

"Perhaps you're right," I said, mildly. "You don't mind if I move about, do you? I'll try not to disturb you."

"Feel free," said Lionel, with typical *bonhomie*. "There's no need for us to sit still or be quiet. There's a long night still ahead of us—plenty of time for the presence to make itself felt more keenly, if it cares to."

"Actually," said Penny, "it might help to pick something up if we turn the lights out."

"It probably would," I agreed. "It would make us more sensitive to the imaginary as well as the real."

She didn't persist with the request, and Martin didn't show the slightest inclination to turn the lights off. It was, after all, his shop, so no one challenged his right to make the decision.

I did a little more shelf-checking, but my heart was no longer in it, and my last faint hopes of finding anything had shriveled way, so I eventually sat down to form a circle of sorts with my three companions.

"What you're feeling," I suggested to them, "is more likely to be atmospheric than paranormal. Even if you leave the anomalous coal-dust from Glofeydd Diafol out of account, moving all the books around and shelving them is bound to have stirred up organic debris of some sort. There's a noticeable odor down here, and odors sometimes have subliminal components that give rise to feelings of slight nausea or unease. Martin's presumably in a position to judge accurately that it's not as noticeable now as it was previously, so it's surely possible that it will disappear completely once the shop's been aired for a day or two and properly vacuumed."

"That's not implausible," Lionel put in, "and it's probably sensible to look for natural explanations before going on to the supernatural ones."

"Unfortunately," Penny said, "I have to agree. Much as I'd like to discover evidenced of a genuine paranormal presence here, I have to concede that what I actually feel at present could well be a slight nausea caused by something material in the air."

"Which doesn't necessarily mean that it's not interesting," I pointed out, dutifully. "The unusual coal from Glofeydd Diafol might well warrant the kind of analysis that a modern mass spectrometer can supply, to see whether there's anything unique among its impurities. Even very simple organic molecules can produce marked psychotropic effects, including methane, and other possible pollutants, like nitrous oxide, can have quite dramatic effects. It wouldn't be at all surprising if people working down pits did see things occasionally, including quite elaborate tricks of the mind."

"Which is not to say," Penny put in, "that all paranormal phenomena can be dismissed as 'mere tricks of the mind.' We mustn't lose sight of the fact that there really are more things in heaven and earth than are dreamt of in a purely materialistic philosophy."

"Amen to that," Lionel added.

"Well," Martin conceded, albeit grudgingly, "If a couple of days of letting the dust settle, airing out the rooms an' some serious elbow-grease with the vac really will get rid of the problem, I'll certainly be happy to do the work. Going to be difficult to persuade the wife, though…an' it might be best to have the exorcism as well, just to be on the safe side."

I wasn't entirely sure that performing exorcisms really did qualify as "the safe side" in terms of potential mental health issues, but that wasn't my call.

Lionel was right, of course, about there being a long stretch of night still ahead of us. I did my bit, and never closed my eyes for a moment.

For a while, I chatted to Lionel about anything and everything except religion. We remembered a few old times and a few old friends; he told me all about *Fortean TV* and I told him about all the stories and articles I'd written lately. I expect the others found it more than a little boring, although Lionel kept bringing them into the conversation at every possible opportunity. He likes to be the life and soul of every party, and he sometimes succeeds in that, even when it seems to be an uphill struggle. He was the commanding presence in the bookshop during that interval; his was the personality that filled it.

All the while, I watched the three of them. I watched them watching the surroundings, waiting for something that always seemed to be on the brink of arriving but never quite did. For a while, at least, they still seemed to feel echoes of a darker presence—of that I was sure, although they made no elaborate attempt to describe or discuss it—but they had no idea what it was. They would probably have liked it to become more clamorous, not so much because that would reveal it more fully and more clearly, but because they thought that the clamor might somehow contain its own explanation—but it wouldn't oblige.

It seemed to all of them, I think, that Martin's hope that a little patience and cleanliness would be the crucial virtues overcoming the presence might well be justified. The brief hold that the liminal presence had exerted on the atmosphere of the shop was loosening by degrees, perhaps simply by virtue of our human presence; it needed no exorcism to persuade it to slip away into oblivion. Hour by hour and inch by inch, Martin's haunted bookshop seemed to me to be becoming *dispirited*.

So far as I could tell, we did nothing to encourage the slow decay of the presence, but we did nothing to prevent it. None of us had the least idea how to encourage it, and three of us would have not wanted to do so had we known how. In the absence of such assistance, it seemed to give up and go away.

As the night dragged on wearily to its end I watched my three companions become sleepier as habit tested their resolve. I heard their voices slow and slur as dreams reached out for them even while they struggled to stay awake—but wakefulness won the war, and the dreams that might have claimed them had they been alone evaporated into the increasingly empty air. The dust stirred up by Martin's exertions and my excursion upstairs was already beginning to settle out and to settle down, adsorbed on to the surfaces of walls and windows, carpets and ceilings. Even when I had first sat down the air had no longer qualified as vintage air; as the morning progressed it became flatter and more insipid, increasingly soured by the faint odors of living flesh.

By the time dawn broke, Martin and Penny were agreed that the presence had gone—that its hold was broken. Martin was slightly anxious that it might return as soon as it could find him on his own again, but Lionel assured him that he would be more than willing to come back if Martin thought it necessary, and would be happy to spend the night alone on the premises if that was the only way to bring the presence out. The way he said it told me that he didn't expect any such thing to occur; without quite knowing why, he seemed convinced that the presence had loosened its grip and lost its hold.

We all had breakfast in a local cafe before the three of us who were returning to Cardiff set forth. Lionel drank lots of black coffee to make sure that he was in no danger of falling asleep at the wheel, although he was no stranger to all-night vigils.

"By the way," Lionel said to Penny and me, after Martin had said his goodbyes and returned to the shop. "A couple of other people have asked me to recruit subjects for an experiment they're doing, and I wondered whether the two of you might be interested."

"What sort of experiment?" I asked, warily. Lionel has fingers in a lot of pies, very few of which are the run-of-the-mill steak-and-kidney variety, so I was ready for almost anything.

"It's all above board," he assured me. "The people in charge have degrees from respectable universities, in psychology and computer science, and they're based at the University of Glamorgan."

The University of Glamorgan had once refused even to interview me for a job teaching creative writing, and in 1997 they were the only university in the UK to attempt to offer a degree in science fiction, so I didn't find that particular item of news at all reassuring.

"I'll take your word for it," I said, patiently, "but what is the experiment supposed to test, and what does it actually entail? My one invariable principle regarding experiments is that if there are needles involved, I'm not."

"They're experimenting with sensory stimuli on brain waves," he said, blandly. "No drugs involved; just music, I think, although I only know the vague outlines. Axel—he's the computer scientist—has written a program that analyzes electric reactions in the brain to various stimuli, and then works out how to reorganize the stimuli so as to provoke a hypnotic state."

"I'm the world's worst hypnotic subject," I told him. "My mother was a hypnotherapist for many years before she retired to Spain, and she'll give me a reference if you ask her. Mind like a nuclear bunker. Suggestibility, on any scale you care to name, absolute zero."

"I know," he said. "That's partly why I thought of you. Axel and Claire asked me to try to find them a spectrum of subjects, ranging from the most credulous to the most skeptical. In the latter category, yours was the first name that came to mind."

"I hope that mine wasn't the first that came to mind at the other extreme," said Penny, gearing up to feel insulted.

"Certainly not," said Lionel, "but they need people in the middle as well, and a serious researcher who has a scrupulously open mind will probably be ideal. They'll need people with fertile imaginations, obviously, but they'll also need people to provide a check on whatever they might come up with. You have a lot of academic knowledge concerning the farther reaches of the human mind that might be very useful as background."

"Why fertile imaginations?" I was quick to ask. "What exactly to they want to do once they've used their fancy software to induce a hypnotic trance."

"Claire doesn't like the term *trance*," Lionel hedged. "From what I gather, they're attempting to reach the collective unconscious...Alex calls it the Comic Mind, and is quick to say that he's not talking about God in the commonly understood sense of the term, although, in my view, of course, he is."

"They're trying to use induced hypnosis to get in touch with God?" said Penny, sounding every bit as skeptical as me."

"Well, no," said Lionel. "That's just my interpretation. Claire and Alex prefer terms like *the implicate order* and *the collective unconscious*, although I think that Alex has found *Cosmic Mind* more useful in trying to explain his theory in simple terms to the volunteers on whom he's already tested his system. That preliminary phase is over now, though, and they're ready to do a properly framed and rigorously monitored experiment."

As a one-time teacher of methodology, I had severe doubts as to whether Alex and Claire's experiment would measure up to my standards of experimental propriety, but that was a minor issue. The more important point was that what they seemed to be doing, according to Lionel's vague report, sounded interesting—at least as interesting, to me, as a haunted bookshop. Penny seemed equally intrigued.

On the other hand, I thought, not only did I consider myself immune to hypnotism, but as someone who not only didn't believe in the Cosmic Mind but would continue to disbelieve in it even if I were staring it in the face. I couldn't imagine that I would be an ideal subject...but every conscientious experiment needs a kind of control sample.

"I'll need more detail before I agree," I said.

"Me too," said Penny.

"Of course," Lionel agreed. "Alex or Claire will ring you, if you're agreeable and can obviously give you a better idea than I can of what's involved—but can I tell them that you're agreeable in principal to the idea of taking part?"

I was about to say yes when another idea struck me. "They're not going to put us in a sensory deprivation tank, are they?" I asked, warily.

"I don't think they could afford one," Lionel said, "but I think their method does involve a measure of sensory deprivation."

"What do you man by a *measure* of sensory deprivation?" I queried.

"I don't know every detail, as I say," he explained, "but you'll be fully briefed beforehand if you want to take part. I doubt if it's more complicated than a blindfold and earphones—as I say, they use music to assist them to obtain the hypnotic state, which they monitor by means of electrodes attached to the outside of the skull. Can I a least give them your telephone number so that they can make their own pitch? You really would be an asset to them. If they only do the experiment with the kind of people who readily line up for that kind of adventure, there's a danger that the results will all look like self-delusion. It's difficult enough as it is to get this kind of work through any kind of peer review."

Penny looked slightly dubious, now that I'd raised the sensory deprivation question, and was obviously mulling it over.

"I didn't know *The Fortean Times* used a peer review system," I said, playing it for laughs while I thought it over myself. "Although I suppose it's the only journal in the world that could run its articles past Sir Isaac Newton, Mothman, and Beelzebub. If the Cosmic Mind signs up for the team, though, I suppose you can dispense with the small fry."

"Very funny," said Lionel. "Can I tell them that the two of you are interested? They'll pay your train fare to Pontypridd and back for the preliminary investigation, plus overnight accommodation and a fifty pound fee. It's not much, I know, but…"

"But if it works I might get to chat with the Cosmic Mind," I finished for him. "Who knows what we might have in common? I hope he doesn't want me to put him in a book, though—I'm a serious skiffy writer. Did I say *he?* I meant *she*, of course. Or *it*. Or…."

Penny interrupted to say: "When?" apparently having finished mulling, obligingly covering up the fact that I hadn't thought of a punch line for the sarcastic monologue.

"The timetable can be fixed to suit you," Lionel said. "It won't be for at least a week, but after that, you can probably book the slot that's most convenient."

"There's no harm in listening to the pitch," I said, giving in, "but I will need more details before making a final decision."

"Me too," Penny agreed, "but it does sound like the sort of thing the Society ought to be interested in, so there's a good chance I'll agree to do it on their behalf, provided that they'll let me report back to the society as well as to them."

"Thanks," said Lionel. "They'll be in touch."

The black coffee had obviously worked, at least until we got to the railway station, where Lionel dropped me off before ferrying Penny back home.

"You didn't have a wasted journey, anyhow," Lionel said, as I got out of the car. He was looking at my overnight bag, which was bulging with the books I'd bought at a pound apiece—a perfectly reasonable price, considering that they were only reading copies—from the parsimonious Martin.

"Not in the least," I said. "To tell you the truth, I don't think any of us did. Sometimes, all it takes to exorcise a presence is to fill a place with people for a while and talk about ordinary matters. Perhaps Martin will feel more at home in the shop from now on."

"Let's hope so," said Lionel. "Thanks for coming down."

I waved goodbye as the car pulled away.

I slept on the train, dreamlessly, all the way back to Reading, and woke up feeling reasonably fit and well in spite of the long night. I had a faint headache and I slight feeling of disorientation, but I put that down to the disruption of my circadian rhythm.

When I got up to leave the train I noticed that the orange upholstery was noticeably stained with black, and felt suitably guilty. I suspected that my jacket would have to go to the dry-cleaners, in spite of the fact that I hadn't taken it upstairs, and I knew that my jeans would definitely have to go into the washing-machine as soon as possible, but I had every faith in the ability of modern technology to clear away the last residues of the dust of Glofeydd Diafol.

Ours is an inhospitable world for matter out of place, I told myself, as I left the station and walked to the bus stop, and, for that matter, mind out of time. Unable to foretell the future, I had no idea of what was to come.

CHAPTER VII

Lionel's friends at the University of Glamorgan were obviously keen, because they certainly didn't waste any time following up his feeler.

I got back to the house at lunchtime, had a quick snack and then went up to the study to work. I was toying with the possibility writing an absurdist comedy called "The Bookworms," in which a high-minded genetic engineer named Bowdler manufactures a new kind of literate worm that eats and excretes ink, with a view to training it to substitute sets of asterisks for expletives. When he's successful, though, other interested parties are quick to move in. Genetic engineers working for the Iranian mullahs start mass producing a subspecies that can convert every text in the world into the *Quran*, forcing the scientific community to close ranks and produce a host of antidote species to reverse the process. Then, natural selection kicks in, and the struggle for intellectual hegemony begins in earnest. The *Quran*-producers soon fall by the wayside because they're unable to adapt, but the ones that colonize the Bible-munching niche soon evolve to the point at which everything from *Genesis* to *Revelation* is converted into trails of excreta representing the complete works of Voltaire, David Hume and Richard Dawkins—which, of course, forces all the Biblical fundamentalists to start singing from a new hymn-sheet. I hadn't actually started, because I still hadn't worked out an ending and strongly suspected that it was far too silly ever to see print, so I wasn't unduly upset when the phone rang.

"Dr. Stableford," said a male voice. "This is Alex Castle, speaking from the psychology department at the University of Glamorgan. Lionel Fanthorpe said that I might call you about our research project."

"He did," I confirmed. "Before I volunteer to be a guinea-pig, though, I'd like to know more about what it entails. I take it that you'll be observing the principle of informed consent, and that you'll at least tell me what you're actually going to do to me, even if you don't go into details about the theory you're testing in case it prejudices my expectations."

"Oh, I don't mind telling you a little bit about the theory," Axel said, blithely. "And the experimental design is really quite simple, although I have to admit that the equipment can seem a trifle intimidating at first glance. We can't afford a full-scale sensory deprivation tank, so it's basically just a comfy chair in a bare room. You'll have headphones, of course, to play the hypnostream and the preliminary music, and we'll tape two halves of a ping pong ball over your eyes to cut out visual stimuli. We'll put an electrode net over your skull, but it'll feel just like a hairnet—nothing heavy."

"Hypnostream?" I queried.

"That's what we call the initial relaxation tape. Lionel tells me that your mother's a hypnotherapist, so you must have heard dozens of them. We'll play that for a little while, until the electroencephalograph tells us you've acquired conscious relaxation; then we'll add in the music, very discreetly. We don't play it loudly, of course—just above the threshold of audibility. There's a further phase, but it's not invasive and it's perfectly harmless, and that doesn't come in until the second session."

"I don't really relax very far," I warned him. "Mind like a steel blade— highly resistant to hypnotic suggestion."

""As I say, the first session only involves conscious relaxation. As for the induced hypnotic state of the second session, you might be surprised. The limited testing we've done suggests that our method of taking a subject down through the various levels of semi-consciousness into a dream-state is highly effective. You do sleep, don't you, Dr. Stableford, so your brain knows perfectly well how to navigate through all the phases of semi-consciousness, even if your mind sometimes refuses to take notice of conventional inducements?"

"I rarely remember my dreams," I told him. *Unless they're about bookshops*, I didn't add, although I certainly thought it. "If you put me to sleep, I probably won't remember a thing when I wake up."

"That's a possibility. We're not aiming for sleep, though, but a particular hypnotic state, objective measurable by brain-wave analysis. Have you ever done any meditation, by any chance?"

"Not seriously. Mostly, I let my endorphins do their own thing. I figure that if I start inducing bliss states on a daily basis I might get addicted to them. A writer needs his presence of mind around the clock—clarity of mind too, if he can manage it, although I will admit that there seem to be plenty of bestsellers who have probably never even got close."

"That's good," he said, amiably. "We're not aiming for a bliss state, as it's sometimes called, but something beyond that. We're trying to reach much more deeply into the primitive parts of the mind than standard meditation techniques, in order to try to establish a more intimate contact with the contents of the collective unconscious."

"Or the Cosmic Mind?"

"If you wish. That's a phrase I find sometimes useful in trying to explain my ideas to lay people, although it's really just a restatement of 'collective unconscious.' It has the advantage of avoiding Jungian paraphernalia, without taking aboard the alternative paraphernalia attached to the idea of God. In brief, yes, we hope that our method of induced hypnosis will enable our subjects to access a part of the mind that isn't individuated and idiosyncratic, but general to the entire human race, and perhaps to the mentality of the universe itself."

It sounded highly dubious to me, but I didn't want to get into a philosophical debate over the phone. There were more down-to-earth issues that required clarification. "What sort of music do you use?" I asked him. "Conventional mood music, I presume—low key muzak?"

"To begin with, but we also try to employ the familiarities and particular tastes of individual subjects. We ask people to bring along some of their own favorite music: something they know well, enjoy and play for their own pleasure. It doesn't have to be particularly relaxing—the main thing is that it's something you like. It's necessary that the second phase of the process relates to artificial rhythms that already have built-in responses in the brain.

"It's an interesting approach," I conceded, although I wasn't at all sure that my favorite music, most of which was Gothic rock, would be ideal for getting in touch with the Comic Mind, if any such thing were possible—which, of course, I doubted extremely.

"It's a vital accessory to the particular hypnotic process with which we're experimenting and the goal we're trying to achieve. Claire's fond of saying that trance and dance equals transcendence."

"I don't dance," I told him, only a trifle frostily. The equation sounded vaguely familiar, but it was more Russell Hoban than Deepak Chopra, so I wasn't entirely unsympathetic. I don't mind life imitating art, so long as it shows a modicum of good taste.

"No, you don't have to." Axel replied, a fraction too earnestly. "You can't actually dance while you're hooked up to the equipment. Not physically, that is. It's more like dancing *inside*. Within the trancing, that is."

I didn't waste any time imaginatively pursuing possible puns on the word trancing, that being the kind of thing best left to the managers of boy bands.

"My favorite music's Goth rock," I warned him. "I think the TM brigade prefer Hindu chants to Fields of the Nephilim."

""I'm not familiar with their work," Alex told me, which completely failed to surprise me, although it showed a dramatic absence of good taste, "but the essential thing is that you have an affinity with it. Music can function as a gateway to alternative states of consciousness, with the right guidance. Once the electroencephalograph has measured your responses to familiar music, it will then be in a position to synthesize a soundscape that guides the neuronal responses. It takes a while, I'm afraid, and will require more than one session, but with the computer power now available to us and the synth equipment, our program ought to be able to design a musical sequence specifically for you, that will hopefully enable your brain to open pathways to the depths of the unconscious."

"Opening the doors of perception?" I queried.

He understood the reference. "It's not a matter of psychedelic tripping," he said. "We're hoping to produce more focused and more consistent results than the old LSD experiments, which I think of as being more like haphazard explosions of mental fireworks than controlled odysseys in the collective unconscious. We're not presuming the accuracy of the detailed Jungian analysis of the archetypes of the unconscious, although it will be interesting if we do locate some of his archetypes. We're endeavoring to keep an open mind about what the contents of the collective unconscious might be and the way they operate, in relation to consciousness on the one hand, and their collective and universal aspects on the other. We can talk more about the background to the project when you're here, of course, but I hope I've told you enough for you to be able to decide whether or not to come aboard."

It did sound harmless, and also intriguing. "Okay," I said. "I'll sign up. When do you want me? I'm perfectly flexible, being self-employed and not actually engrossed at the present."

"That's great. We should have everything set up and ready to go by the end of the week, and we'll do a few final test runs over the weekend and launch the experiment proper on Monday. Would Tuesday afternoon suit you for the first run? You'll need to stay overnight here, but the second run on Wednesday should terminate the experimental run, and you can be back home that evening, if that's satisfactory."

"It's fine," I assured him. "How many CDs should I bring along?"

"Four should be entirely adequate, but you can bring along a couple of extra ones if you want. Lionel Fanthorpe will be here doing sessions on Monday and Tuesday morning, and he's volunteered to meet you at Pontyprydd station, drive you to the hotel and then bring you out to the lab, if you can let him know what time your train arrives."

"Will do," I said, unsurprised that Lionel had volunteered to be guinea-pig number one.

"I'll see you a week today, then," he said, sounding full of youthful enthusiasm.

"Okay," I said. "Notify the Cosmic Mind to expect me, and not to be too intimidated by my reputation."

I hung up, and then began to wonder whether I'd done the right thing.

It seemed, in one sense, likely to be a useful distraction. Telling the amiable Axel that I wasn't seriously engrossed at the moment had been a drastic understatement. Not only wasn't I seriously engrossed but I was having considerable difficulty settling down to anything. Even relatively brief articles such as the introduction to the Pamely collection that I'd done a few days before, were proving unusually taxing.

I was seriously annoyed with that, because it wasn't as if I hadn't been left by one of my wives before. The Ex had dragged the process out for an excruciating year, and although **** tended to disappear much more abruptly, she also tended to change her mind after a matter of months, weeks, or even days. In the five years since she had left me for the first time I'd already lost count of the times she had repeated the disappearing act, although the present absence was only the third time that she'd actually moved all of her ever-diminishing possessions out of the house, leaving nothing behind but a gap. I should, in theory, have been used to it by now, and capable of simply working through it—and, indeed, of using work as a means of focusing my attention and absorbing my concentration. In practice, though, it wasn't that straightforward.

As I say, I was appalled by my own fragility, but being appalled by it wasn't the same as being able to deny it. The patent fact was that I was a bit of a wreck at that particular moment in time, and although I had been able to maintain a reasonably brave face while doing my stint in Martin's bookshop, and had been able to employ the episode as the kind of distraction that I probably needed, the prospect of a sensory deprivation experiment in which some kind of computer program was first going to probe my brain in order to explore its particular sensitivities and then use them to open up channels of thought that were usually sealed off—perhaps for good reasons—seemed a trifle more challenging. However, I was sufficiently proud of my carefully-cultivated reputation for stubborn hard-headedness not to be reluctant to test my actual psychological defenses, even while I knew that they were under stress. I wasn't sure that it was the ideal time to be making attempts to peer into the abyss, and allowing the abyss a chance to peer into me, but precisely because I wasn't sure, I didn't want to back down from the challenge.

The thought that it might actually do me good, as a cheap alternative to lying on a shrink's couch, never occurred to me; I had always held firm to the opinion that I wouldn't lay on a shrink's couch even if he paid me, on the grounds that a true Yorkshireman does not suffer fools gladly, and I took it for granted that all psychoanalysts, of whatever stripe, were *ipso facto* fools. At least Axel Castle had made one decisively good move by dismissing the existing fantasies of Jungian thought and claiming to be going deep-psyche diving with an open mind as to what he might find. I wasn't at all convinced that I believed him, especially given his fondness for the idea of the Cosmic Mind, but the fact that he was willing to make the effort to pretend was a point in his favor.

After some thought, however, I decided that there was probably no risk. It wasn't as if the electroecephalograph would be able to read my mind. All that Axel Castle would ever know about what I experienced under the stimulus of his synthesized music track was what his instruments recorded and whatever I cared to tell him. Not that I was anticipating having anything to tell him that would be in the least discomfiting, or that I was planning to lie—but knowing that I had the last redoubt of blatant deception available to me seemed a safety-net of sorts, in the unlikely event that I might need one.

I didn't start the bookworm story; indeed, I discarded the idea as unworkable even as an exercise in humorous absurdism, and tried to think of something else instead.

Usually, that wasn't too difficult; I'd never been overly prone to writer's block, and if I'd had some commissioned non-fiction on hand I'd surely have been able to throw myself into it with a certain method even if I lacked enthusiasm, but I was left to my own devices. At least I had my usual stack of books for evaluation piled up—I was a judge for one of the annual science fiction awards at the time, which compelled me to keep on reading at least forty or fifty candidate novels a year—albeit mostly without enthusiasm. In 1997 I was still a couple of years away from the point at which the deterioration of my eyesight forced me to give up such work, but it was already becoming a bit of a strain.

At any rate, that was how I spend the latter part of the afternoon.

I didn't eat until late, but the delay didn't allow me to build up much of an appetite, and when I'd finished I couldn't find anything on television that I could actually bear the idea of watching, so I decided to go back to reading simply for something to do. I still had a faint headache, and still felt slightly disorientated, but there was nothing wrong with me that I would have qualified as being ill—merely slightly *off color*. Given my situation, ****-wise, it would have been more surprising if I hadn't felt off color. When depression and obsession are your natural states of mind, as they had always been mine, you have relatively low standards for what actually qualifies as feeling well.

I went back into the front room, sat down on the sofa, and reached out for the book that I'd left on the coffee-table—but I never picked it up, because that's when I saw the Devil.

CHAPTER VIII

It wasn't dark yet, and the sun hadn't actually set, although it was low on the horizon. There was no possibility, therefore, that he was just a trick of the gloom. He was sitting in the armchair, quite relaxed.

I knew who he was, and never had a moment's doubt about it, although I can't say exactly how it was that I know. I had never seen him before, and he didn't look like any of his conventional representations, but I recognized him immediately. I *knew* him. He wasn't unduly tall—maybe five-ten or so—and he didn't have any conventional paraphernalia along the lines of horns, a beard or even piercing eyes; indeed his gaze was mild and slightly amused. He was handsome without being movie-star handsome, and dressed in a casual dark gray lounge-suit with a cream shirt; his one concession to sartorial flamboyance was a crimson cravat.

A number of questions went through my head, but I didn't voice any of them. I'm not often left speechless, but I think that finding the Devil in your front room without him having bothered to open the door, let alone telephone in advance, qualifies as the kind of occasion that might have that effect.

It was therefore left to him to break the ice, which he did by saying: "Have you got anything to drink?"

I suspected that he didn't mean tea.

"Only red wine," I said.

"I suppose that'll do, if you haven't got anything stronger," he conceded. "You wouldn't care to open a bottle, by any chance, would you? I need a drink."

I felt in need of a little pick-me-up myself. The wine-rack was in the kitchen. I went to get a bottle, a corkscrew and two glasses.

I half-expected that the Devil might have vanished by the time I got back, as a more discreet hallucination might have done, but he was still there when I returned with a bottle of Pinot Noir. He watched me uncork the bottle and pour a reasonable measure into each of the two glasses.

I took a sip before saying: "To what do I owe the pleasure?"

"Is it a pleasure?" he asked, slightly surprised.

"I was just being polite," I told him, although it might have been more honest to say sarcastic "I suppose that there's no point in asking you whether I'm asleep and dreaming, because I wouldn't be able to believe you if you said no."

"You're not asleep," he assured me, "and there's no reason why you shouldn't believe me."

"And I haven't gone mad, either?" I said, just to check.

"You're perfectly sane," he informed me, "in spite of the obsession and the depression."

"Okay," I said. "So if this isn't a dream and I'm not mad, let me ask again: to what exactly, to I owe the fact that I'm sitting in my front room talking to the non-existent Devil?"

"I didn't say that you're not dreaming," he pointed out, "I only said that you're not asleep. The simplest answer to your question is that you owe my presence to the psychotropic dust that you inhaled in such considerable quantities yesterday, and the association you made in your imagination between the carbonaceous materials therein and the ideas derived from the nickname of the pit."

"So I am dreaming?" I asked, uncertainly.

"Yes and no," he replied. "You knew as soon as you stepped into the upstairs room in the bookshop that the relevant states of consciousness had begun to overlap. Clearly, the overlap is intensifying, and becoming more intricately confused. It's an interesting situation, if you think about it—and an opportunity, of course, which you might not have again."

Watching him sip liquid wine from a solid glass made him appear perfectly material, as hallucinations go, but matter, as every Berkeleyan knows, is the possibility of sensation, so there didn't seem to be any reason to unduly surprised by his apparent solidity.

"You are just a figment of my imagination, then?" I asked him, warily.

"That is one way of looking at it," he conceded.

"You don't actually exist, though," I suggested, accusatively.

"I do and I don't," he countered. "But for the moment, at least, you might do well to accept the working hypothesis that there's a sense in which I do, even if the question of what I am remains open."

"Now I know that you're a figment of my imagination," I said. "Nobody I know talks like that, except me."

"I do," he replied.

"But even if there's a sense in which you do exist," I probed, "it's not the same sense in which I exist, is it?" I guessed even before I'd completed the observation, though, what response I was going to get.

"Oh," he informed me, not without a certain smug self-satisfaction. "I exist far more reliably than *that*. Whereas you're ephemeral, I'm eternal; whereas your existence is continually interrupted by periods of unconsciousness, I never cease to exist; and whereas you're hardly the same from one day to the next, I'm far less fickle and far more disciplined in my metamorphoses."

I supposed that I ought to be grateful for the fact that he hadn't pointed out that practically the entire human race was ignorant of my existence, whereas they all knew about him, in one guise or another. I didn't want to get into a quiddity context, though.

"You never sleep?" I queried, instead.

"Never," he confirmed.

"You and God both, then," I remarked, assuming that all his arguments for his own existence would also apply to the thesis whose antithesis he was.

"Technically, yes," he agreed, "but I don't have His capacity for prolonged inattention, so it might be argued that I'm more awake than He is." I admired the way in which he emphasized the pronouns, to make their reference unmistakable.

"Indeed?" I queried. "But all the Biblical and apocryphal imagery related to the two of you is just fantasy, right?"

"Not all of it," he said.

"You really did get thrown out of heaven for the sin of pride, then, and condemned to supervise punishments in Hell?"

"Not exactly," he said. "There was a slight but inevitable philosophical dispute between the two of us, which did result in accusations of pride being thrown around, but there is no Hell of eternal punishments."

"That's a relief," I said, although it wasn't an anxiety I'd ever seriously entertained, so I really couldn't have expected any Devil summoned up from the depths of my mind by a psychotropic intervention to endorse the notion. "You're not here to make a pact with me, then?"

"Of course I am," he replied, serenely, and took a sip of wine before adding: "Why else would I be here?"

"You're actually here to bargain for my soul?" I said, incredulously.

"Oh, no," he said, in a voice that might have been intended to sound reassuring rather than contemptuous, although, after another sip of Pinot Noir, he went on to add, serenely: "You know as well as I do how little that's worth."

"I've read my Edgar Allan Poe," I told him. "I'm certainly not going to bet you my head."

He looked at me slightly askance, then, and said: "What is it, then, that you think you're doing?"

I was taken slightly aback, but I decided to treat it as a serious question, because it was, I realized, quite an important one. What did I think I was doing? Or, at least, what did I think was happening to me?

"I think I'm hallucinating," I told him.

"And?" he prompted, inviting me to recognize the inadequacy of the answer.

"And...I'm not exactly certain yet. I guess there's a sense in which I must be debating with myself, reflecting my own anxieties, momentary and existential, and that I've produced you as a kind of foil so that I can hold a discussion with myself, perhaps encouraged by the fact that I've just been invited to make contact with your counterpart, although the experimenter calls him the Cosmic Mind rather than God."

"I don't call Him that either," he observed.

"And given all that," I said, continuing my open train of thought, for the benefit of clarification, "for all your claims to a more secure and elaborate existence than I have, you're just a fragment of my identity. You aren't an independent individual genuinely capable of striking bargains. You can't actually offer me anything, or take anything from me in exchange, can you?"

"Yes I can," he said, simply. "I do have something to offer and I do want something in exchange."

"What?" I snapped back.

I was expecting him to say: "What do you want?" because I thought that was the point of the hallucinatory discussion we were having. I thought that I had to be interrogating myself in some sense, trying to ask myself difficult questions and recruiting the Devil to do it because he was slightly easier to entertain than Him, alias the Cosmic Mind.

For the moment, though, he wasn't prepared to be that blunt. If that was really what he was all about, if that was really why I'd summoned him—assuming that, in some sense, I had summoned him, albeit without being consciously aware of it—he wanted to work up to it by a roundabout route.

What he actually said was: "May I tell you a story?"

Perhaps I should have expected that. I'm a writer, after all, and at that point in time I was a writer in temporary difficulties, what else could I ask of the Devil more urgently than that he tell me a story?

"Please do," I said.

So he did.

"Let me say right away," he said, "that I had nothing whatsoever to do with the death of Toby Dammit. If people want to see something of the 'irony of fate' in the fact that he lost his head after declaring his wager, that's up to them, but it was really just one of those things: an accident with a hint of ironic coincidence. There is no fate. Things are not 'meant to be,' ironically or otherwise. They just are. Anyway, people bet me their heads all the time, albeit more often tacitly than explicitly, and I always leave their heads on their shoulders when I win, where they can be of some use to me. I would never dream, in a million years, of collecting on such a bet by means of crude mortal violence. That's not my style.

"You can take my word for that. I always tell the truth. That's why addicts of deceptive faith call me the Father of Lies, and cynics the Imp of the Perverse.

"If you want my advice, in fact—and you really should, because there's no one better qualified to offer it—you'll keep on betting me your head, tacitly if not explicitly. That's what a head is for. If you aren't willing to wager your intellect on questions of good and evil, by making real and hypothetical awkward moral judgments, what kind of pathetic excuse for a human being are you? You should *always* bet the Devil your head, and I'm perfectly sincere in wishing you the best of luck, because I'm a sportsman, and I know how heavily the house percentage is weighed in my favor.

"What you really shouldn't do, of course, if you value your soul, is bet the Devil your heart. That really is foolish, because that kind of bet, you really can't win. I'd take no pleasure in the inevitability of your losing, not merely because there's no pleasure in facile triumph, but because I don't have the capacity to feel it, even though I have a heart myself. I'm a bad person, I know—by definition—but I couldn't be half as bad as I am if I didn't have a heart. I've bet my own heart and lost, so I know what it feels like. I know the measure of tragedy, albeit only intellectually, better than anyone.

"But enough boring philosophical commentary; I'm supposed to be telling you a story.

"It happened in New Orleans, back in the early nineteenth century. It was my favorite haunt in the Americas in those days, although not a patch on Paris. I appreciated the tombs, carefully erected above the water table, which filled the entire city with the reek of decay and the phosphorescence of putrescence. I appreciated the city's eccentric Mardi Gras celebrations—although not as much as Venice's, obviously—and I appreciated Voudun, which was in the early days of it development then. And I appreciated the decadence—the decadence, perhaps, most of all. That's the way my es-thetic sensibilities are orientated.

"I was staying with a local planter named Jacques Lacroix, to whom I'd obtained a letter of introduction from one of his factors in Marseilles. At least, 'Jacques Lacroix' was what he called himself in America; he'd had a different name when he lived in France, and had ended up in the Conciergerie under the Convention and was fortunate to be released by the Directoire. He'd been lucky to escape the guillotine. He was one of the rare immigrants who really had made his fortune in the colonies, rising from humble origins to be the owner of a large estate, a fine house and more than three hundred slaves. Like most slave-owners who'd been little better than a slave himself at one time, he wasn't a gentle master, but he wasn't the worst either. He understood that it was good idea to keep the people on whom his fortune depended in good health, and reasonable comfort.

"If there really were a Hell, it would probably have a special circle for slave-owners—obviously, if there had ever been a Hell it would have had to expand its accommodations vastly since Dante's day—and another for slaves; the former would presumably not be glad of the fact, but the latter probably would, even if some of them were disappointed about not getting into Heaven. They wouldn't be disappointed if they knew the truth, of course, but they don't, and they wouldn't believe me if I told them.

"Lacroix had two other guests staying with him at the time. One of them was an old friend—or an old acquaintance, at least, who made his living, when he wasn't spending his ill-gotten gains, as a pirate—although he preferred the term 'corsair.' His name had once been Jean Dupré, but he naturally preferred to be known in Louisiana as Dupree, and liked to style himself 'Dancing Jack' Dupree, because every pirate named Jean, John or Johan liked to style himself 'Dancing Jack.' Pirates tend to copy one another relentlessly, because it's the only way they know how to go about being a pirate; there isn't a guide-book. When he laid low he usually dropped anchor the secret inlets of the Mississippi delta rather than joining the gang in Tortuga, because he had too many enemies among his own kind.

"Dupree wasn't really a corsair, of course, in the sense that he'd ever obtained a warrant from Napoléon to harass English shipping—he attacked anyone at all, provided that they were unlikely to fight back—but he liked the idea of being a Romantic figure rather than treacherous brute. Ashore, he posed as a dandy, and was relentless in his pursuit of women. He'd probably committed more rapes than Lacroix, although I don't have any exact account-books to hand. That's just the way of the world, of course, but it has to be admitted that Dupree had also slept with more willing women than Lacroix, and I don't just mean whores. When he was on song, the dandy act sometimes paid off.

"The third guest at the Lacroix House that season was a young Northerner named Abraham Cardingly. He was in the South to do business, representing a manufacturer of agricultural equipment, but the reason he'd been given the job was that he had relatives in the region, albeit distant ones. He was second cousin to Lacroix's wife, and although they hadn't ever met before he'd struck up a relationship of sorts by mail, which had proved adequate to save him from the kind of hotel-based existence to which most commercial representatives from the North were condemned.

"Lacroix liked playing the host; he felt that it gave him status and prestige, as well as relieving the boredom. He was one of those men who'd been all energy and ambition while striving to make his fortune, but who didn't quite know what to do with himself once he'd got it, and liked to have guests in order to have witnesses to assure him that the struggle had been worthwhile and the prize worth winning. In fact, he liked playing host so much that he might have knowingly offered hospitality to the Devil himself, although I'm too polite ever to ask that of a man, no matter how many favors he might owe me. I was making that particular trip under the pseudonym of Savinien de Monfort, although I was careful to disclaim close relationship with the other branches of the family. I represented myself as a traveler for pleasure and education, which was partly true, from Paris, which was also partly true in the sense that I know the city well and have always thought of it as a kind of spiritual home—far more so, at any rate, than any imaginary Pandemonium.

"Naturally, Jacques Lacroix had a beautiful daughter named Lucile. I say naturally, because there wouldn't be a story if there weren't a beautiful daughter—not, at least, a story told under the rubric of 'Never Bet the Devil Your Heart,' which, if I forgot to mention it, is the title of this one. Equally naturally, she caught the eye of both Abraham Cardingly and Jack Dupree, albeit in somewhat different ways. Cardingly was a Northerner of Puritan descent, if not Puritan inclinations, and his intentions, vague as they were while he wallowed in youthful confusion, were entirely honorable. Jack Dupree's were not.

"I don't mean to suggest that Dupree would ever have considered raping Lucile; he wasn't an honorable man, by any stretch of the imagination, but he knew the value of hospitality, especially to a pirate. Raping a white girl might have closed the entirety of New Orleans to him forever. Seduction, however, was another matter; if he succeeded, Jacque Lacroix wouldn't like it a bit, and he'd never be invited back to that particular residence—but everyone else would find it rather amusing, and it would only add to his reputation as 'Dancing Jack.'

"Again, let me say that I'm not responsible for that is any way whatsoever. Things are the way they are. It's not my fault. I have a role to play, that's all. I didn't cast lustful eyes at Lucile Lacroix myself. It would be ludicrous to deny that I'm a seducer of sorts—I have my role to play—but I'm not the kind of seducer that Jack Dupree was ambitious to be, and in which capacity he had some success. Lust isn't one of my deadly sins.

"Having said that, though, I do take a pride in my appearance when I put on mortal flesh. I'm always handsome. You've probably heard different, but most of that is just Church propaganda. When it comes to politics, the Church always goes negative and is never content with half-measures. You really shouldn't believe the things they say about me, any more than you should believe what they say about Hell, but I must admit that I don't fight back on that score. For one thing, it's beneath my dignity, and for another, it actually makes it easier to play my role if people are loaded down with silly and slanderous preconceptions. I don't say I've never manifested myself with hooves, horns and a tail, but I've only ever done it to put the wind up Churchmen, in a spirit of good humor. For all normal purposes, I'm handsome. I suppose, in my way, I'm a bit of a dandy—but not like Jack Dupree, or even Lord Byron.

"Now there's a man who bet me his heart, with disastrous consequences—but that's another story.

"The nub of *this* story is that it really wasn't my fault that Lucile Lacroix took it into her head to fall in love with me and not with Abraham Cardingly or Jack Dupree. I did nothing to encourage her, and had the situation been simpler, I might have been able to let her down gently and courteously, with no harm done. It wasn't my fault, either, that Jacques Lacroix took it into his head to agree wholeheartedly with his daughter's 'choice' and make his sympathy known to her largely because he didn't want Dupree or Cardingly turning her head.

"Had I not been there, I suspect that one of the others might have turned her head, because they were certainly trying hard. Cardingly had a romanticized view of the South and its legendary belles, and he thought that he had some kind of claim on Lucile because she was a distant cousin. He didn't know the details of Jack Dupree's career, but he didn't need any help from local gossip to judge what kind of man the pirate was, and that doubtless made him doubly anxious to 'save' Lucile from the danger of seduction by such an out-and-out scoundrel. He had nothing against me, of course but he seemed to think that because I was Dupree's fellow-guest, we must be birds of a feather, and my prepossessing exterior only made him more suspicious of my presumed deceptiveness.

"Not unnaturally, Dupree's awareness of Cardingly's interest only added spice to his own; the opportunity to give an honest Northerner a poke in the eye as well as have his wicked way with an innocent virgin whose hormones had only just started to rage was a truly juicy prize in his eyes. Dupree was under no delusions about the similarity of his plumage to mine, but he didn't quite know what to make of me. He was well aware of Lucile's interest in me, but as soon as he had observed that it was unreciprocated, he dismissed me as a significant rival, and judged me irrelevant to his own quest—at least initially.

"As I said, none of that was my fault. Nor was it my fault that as time wore on and the days of our residence at the Lacroix House turned into weeks, the combination of circumstances just described gradually filled Cardingly and Dupree with two different varieties of bitter disappointment, tending towards two different varieties of angry desperation. Neither of them made any headway, and both perceived that they were unlikely to make any while I was in the picture, in spite of my diffidence, which only seemed to inflame Lucile's infatuation with me, and her father's approval of it.

"To tell the truth, I wasn't tempted to bring my planned departure forward in order to ease the situation, not just because I still had business to do in the city but because there was a certain amusement in watching my two fellow guests become increasingly fretful, angry with themselves as well as everyone else. I really didn't think that the matter would come so swiftly to a head; I can't foresee the future, although my judgments of its likelihood are inevitably more reliable than most. I knew that such rivalries have a synergy that increases their toxicity, but, being calm and rational person myself, I sometimes underestimate the foolish lengths to which humans can be driven by frustrated passion.

"Not unnaturally, it was Jack Dupree who came up with the idea that if he could somehow put me out of the picture, Cardingly wouldn't be likely to put up sufficient competition to stop him reaching his goal. He would gladly have shot me in the back, of course, and dumped my body in the swamp—much good it would have done him!—but he still had enough presence of mind to know that it would be better by far approach the problem in a different way. He mulled it over for a while, and then came up with a plan of sorts. My relatively modest habits had convinced him that I wasn't a rich man, and might well be vulnerable to financial disaster.

"With that thought in mind, Dupree suggested a card game, intending to cheat—intending to cheat me, that is; he had no intention of dishonestly taking money off his host, and had no particular designs in Cardingly, because he knew that it would look suspicious if he pauperized us both.

"Cardingly didn't want to play; he wasn't a gambler by nature. He was, however, a stranger in a strange land, and he wasn't entirely sure what the etiquette of such situations was, and Dupree was careful to insinuate, with all the subtlety of which he was capable, that it wouldn't be polite for him to refuse, and might well be seen as a failure of courage, especially by Mademoiselle Lacroix.

"Lacroix didn't really want to play either, probably because he wasn't entirely convinced that it was a good idea to play cards with a man like Jack Dupree, even if you were his host—but Dupree had known Lacroix for a long time, and deep down, the two of them were birds of a feather, so he contrived to talk him round. If he was surprised at my lack of reluctance, he didn't show it; he was too eager to be suspicious.

"At any rate, the eventual result of Dupree's secret scheming was that the four of us sat down on the veranda one evening after dinner, with a couple of bottles of what claimed to be Cognac between us, ready to make a night of it. Lucile was eager to watch, not because she was interested in the esthetics of gambling, but because it gave her an opportunity to gaze longingly at me. I'd been absent in the city for most of the previous forty-eight hours, and her poor amorous eyes were feeling starved.

"I had no objection at all to playing, of course; I'll even admit to being enthusiastic—but what I was enthusiastic about was the prospect of a duel of wits with Jack Dupree. Like him, I regarded the other two as neutrals, not targets. Unlike the pirate, I had no intention of cheating—as I said before, I never tell lies, although I do admit to running the occasional double bluff, telling the truth in order to be disbelieved—but I had every intention of using my superior skill and mathematical acumen to demonstrate to him that cheats sometimes lose, and that there's no safety in dishonesty, even in honest company.

"Had I wanted to, I could have ensured that the cards fell in a certain way without employing any actual sleight of hand, but I wouldn't have dreamed of doing so. I'm a sportsman; I was fully committed to letting hazard take its course, however wayward it might be. I was even prepared to lose, if that happened to be the way things turned out. Not only am I a sportsman, but I know that you can sometimes gain more in the greater game by losing in the trivial ones—and *vice versa*.

"As chance would have it, with a little help from some rather inept double-dealing, Dupree did start out winning. So did I, without any assistance but skill. Lacroix lost a little, but most of the loss was taken by Cardingly—who was, I have to say, by no means a serious student of probability. Dupree was far better, and could have wiped the floor with him in an honest game—but that wasn't Dupree's objective, and although he took the money, he became increasingly irritated because he wasn't winning it from the right source. I think that he would actually have started cheating on Cardingly's behalf as well as his own, if it hadn't been for the force of his own greed, and the fact that Lacroix began cheating too.

"All three of them were, of course, very aware of the fact that Lucile was watching, and all three of them were paying as much attention to her as to the game—unwisely, in Cardingly's case, although he probably wouldn't have been doing much better if he were fully focused, Dupree's primary objective—a stupid one, needless to say, even if I had been only human—had been to inflict heavy losses on me in order to make it necessary for me to leave the house, but he had also hoped to humiliate me in Lucile's eyes while making himself look good. He could see readily enough that he was failing all round in that respect; not only was I not on my way to humiliation, but his winnings weren't impressing Lucile in the least. How could they, when she only had eyes for me?

"As for Lacroix, he could see that Dupree was cheating, and even though he could see that he wasn't the intended victim, he didn't want either of his other guests to be robbed by a pirate while they were under his roof, and therefore thought it incumbent on him to fight Dupree's fire with fire of his own. That made the situation even more amusing, and the fact that Lacroix's cheating was aimed specifically at Dupree actually made it easier for me to continue winning by playing honestly—but it also increased the rapidity of Cardingly's losses, initiated by sheer incompetence but now made worse by increasing desperation.

"Had the game gone on long enough, I think that the tide might have turned, and that Lacroix and I between us might have contrived to divert at least some of Dupree's winnings back in his direction. Cardingly, alas, didn't have that kind of patience. He was kind of person who believed that luck somehow owed him a rapid opportunity to redeem his losses by means of his own reckless betting.

"In the next phase of the game, with the combined effects of my skill and Lacroix's sharping, Dupree was only holding his own. He wasn't losing, but he wasn't winning either, and he was beginning to realize that his plan had gone awry, and that he was going to have to come up with another. Lacroix was only winning back what he'd previously lost. The only one materially increasing his fortune was me…and Cardingly was still losing.

"Perhaps I should have paid more heed to the warning when Cardingly growled at me that I had 'the Devil's own luck' when he lost yet another hand on a stupid bet, but I was still focused on Dupree, waiting for a chance to take him down. So it came as a complete surprise when Cardingly suddenly stood up, driven beyond the limits of his endurance by emotional tension and overindulgence in Cognac, and accused me of cheating.

"For a moment, I actually thought that he was talking to Dupree, having spotted the pirate's manipulations, but he wasn't. I saw Dupree laugh, genuinely amused by the fact that the idiot cousin had actually accused the only one of his opponents who wasn't cheating, rather than either of the two who were—and I also saw him smother the laugh immediately, because he understood even better than Cardingly what the effects of that stupidity were bound to be, and knew that it was diplomatically necessary to hide his smug sense of triumph.

"Cardingly did understand, of course; he had no excuse of ignorance. Callow Northerner he might be, but he knew enough about Southern mores to know that he'd just made it inevitable that he and I would have to fight a duel. He wasn't, of course, hoping to kill me in the duel, but he was probably harboring some faint hope of my being obliged to leave thereafter, while he, as a family relative, might be able to stay. That was a delusion, but perhaps an understandable one. The primary reason for his rush of blood was, however, the same as Dupree's reason for cheating: he wanted to diminish me in Lucile's eyes. His judgment of women was as poor as his judgment of cards.

"'Come now, Monsieur Cardingly,' I said, softly, 'You don't really mean that.'

"'I most certainly do,' he said, probably lying—not that it mattered. The die was cast. He would never have made such a bet with his head, but his heart…the heart is essentially foolish; it has no regard for the calculus of probability in the short term or the long.

"What could I do? It didn't seem to me that I had any choice.

"'In fact,' I said, casually, 'I wasn't cheating. Monsieur Dupree was, but I wasn't.' Obviously, I didn't mention my host's dereliction; I always tell the truth, but not always the whole truth. Nobody's perfect—except Him, allegedly, and I have my doubts about Him.

"If Cardingly's declaration had caused a shock, mine more than re-doubled it. They all knew, after all, that I was no idiot, and must have calculated my words exactly. Dupree's expression of restrained satisfaction disappeared, but it was replaced by a predatory gleam in his eye: that of a raptor which has spotted an opportunity. Dupree was a pirate; he fancied himself a swashbuckling swordsman and a ruthless one.

"'Oh dear,' I added, mildly, when no one said a word. 'It seems that I'll have to fight you both, doesn't it? We seem to have a slight shortage of seconds, but I'm sure that we can overlook that formality with a view to a rapid resolution. As the insulted party, Monsieur Cardingly, I believe that I have the choice of weapons for our encounter. Do you have a pair of épées, Monsieur Lacroix?'

"'Of course,' said Lacroix.

"Cardingly was bewildered by the pace at which things were moving, but he consented to be led out to the lawn in front of the house. We were indeed direly short of seconds, but not of an audience. When the word spread through the house that two of the Master's guests were about to have at one another with unbuttoned foils, it only took a matter of moments for a huge ring of black faces to form on the outskirts of the lawn—and Lacroix didn't instruct his overseers to chase them away. He wanted witnesses, just in case he needed to be let off some kind of hook.

"The first duel posed no real difficulty; my one and only priority was to give Dupree the impression that, although I was a better swordsman that the woefully inept Abraham Cardingly, I wasn't nearly as good as him. I know how to hold back, though, and had enough skill to look clumsy while taking no real risks. I spun the fight out for four minutes—four minutes is a long time in a fencing match—to make sure that the lesson went home.

"When I eventually wounded Cardingly in his right forearm, making it impossible for him to continue the fight, I made it look as if had been aiming for his shoulder and missed. I even pretended to be weary, and that nothing but pride was urging me on to fight Dupree immediately. He had the choice of weapons, of course, and thought he was being cunning in putting on a show of negligent generosity is saying that we might as well use the same ones.

"Lucile was still watching, of course, and Dupree knew as well as I did that her admiration for me had only increased thus far, but his new plan was to turn that advantage on its head in spectacular fashion, and perhaps to give me an ugly wound in the process. He too was gambling with his heart rather than his head—an unforgivable error in a man of his dark stripe.

"It probably took Dancing Jack all of ten seconds to realize that he had made a terrible mistake, once he had seen me parry two swift lunges—at which point he became mortally afraid for his life. He had begun the duel intending to play the dandy and the dancer, and eventually to wound me as I had wounded Cardingly, if a little more seriously, but once he realized that he might well be outclassed as a fencer, he attacked with all his might and desperation, trying to kill me. Again, it was not a bet hat he would have made with his head, but he was all heart now, and more thoroughly doomed than before.

"I never even considered killing him. I'm not a murderous person, although I claim no moral credit for that. Who knows better than I how much more torment there is on the real Earth than there is in the imaginary Hell, for a man who has suffered defeat, humiliation and the frustration of his desires? I'm not a murderous person, but I'm not a merciful one either.

"After five minute of cat-and-mouse, I carefully wounded the rapidly-tiring pirate in the leg, not fatally, but badly enough to put his career as a sea-raider in jeopardy and efficiently enough to make sure that he could never again describe himself as 'Dancing Jack' without occasioning hilarity.

"After that, of course, none of us could decently stay in Jacques Lacroix's house. Protocol demanded that we all pack our bags and leave, not because there was the slightest possibility of our being arrested for dueling, but simply because it was the decent thing to do.

"I apologized to my host profusely for the disturbance I had occasioned, but he forgave me readily enough, knowing what I had not said as well as what I had—and knowing, too, that I had done the world a favor in denting Jack Dupree's reputation, and making sure that he would never again seek to take advantage of his old acquaintance to claim hospitality at the Lacroix House.

"It wasn't until I had made my discreet exit from the house—the first to leave because I had no need of medical attention—that the ultimate consequence of my capitulation with the inevitable materialized. I could have foreseen it; perhaps I had, but had simply avoided thinking about it.

"Lucile Lacroix followed me out into the darkness of the night, and begged me to take her with me. She confessed her love—an infatuation boosted to fever pitch by the two duels I had just fought, and which she had imagined, not entirely without reason, to have been fought for her, against two avid suitors whose attentions she had been anxious to avoid.

"'Child,' I said to her, with perfect calm of mind, 'you should not do this. You should not surrender to passion in this way, offering yourself so wholeheartedly to a person you do not know; it is a path that can only lead you, without a long delay, to ignominy and disappointment. You should use your head, your intellect, to fight temptation courageously; your heart will always betray you, will always surrender to foolishness. I am embarked upon my own road, and you should not follow me even if you could.'

"Can anyone imagine, even for a minute, that she would listen to such reason? She begged me; she implored me; she threatened to kill herself if I rejected her. She might even have meant it. She was seriously overwrought.

"What could I do? What, in all conscience, could I do?

"I gave her what she wanted, and took her a little way along the road of eternity. When I left her, without a long delay, to ignominy and disappointment, I tried to do so as gently as unhumanly possibly. I am, as I have said, a bad person—but I appeal to you with, as a person with a level head, who might yet bet against me and win, in that regard: could you, or any unfallen angel, have done any better?"

CHAPTER IX

Why was the Devil telling me that story? Obviously, I listened to it, hanging on his every word, but I never lost sight of that fact that the most remarkable thing about it was the fact of his telling it to me.

I suppose the more fundamental matter was that fact that he was there at all, given that he didn't exist, with the corollary fact that he was sitting there in an extremely good imitation of the flesh drinking actual Pinot Noir left over from my last day trip to Auchan in Boulogne out of a actual glass with an apparent contentment, but I simply had to take that for granted.

Obviously, I was hallucinating, because I'd overdosed on the haunting-juice matured in the bindings and pages of the black books from Glofeydd Diafol while they'd been in storage. Because I'd stubbornly insisted, as only a Yorkshireman can, in taking all the books out of the boxes and opening them one by one to look at their incredibly uninteresting title-pages I'd taken aboard a vastly greater dose than Martin had absorbed while starting the unpacking, which had only given him a creepy sense of alien presence.

The fact that it had taken twenty-four hours to take effect was a trifle peculiar, but probably only signified that my brain had taken time to adapt fully to the alien presence in my blood. As the Devil had kindly pointed out, the overlap in my states of consciousness had actually begun much earlier.

At any rate, he was there, and questions of speculative biochemistry could probably be shelved. The more urgent question was not whether or not he existed but why. What was his paradoxical existence-in-spite-of-non-existence trying to communicate to me—because, quite obviously, it was trying to communicate something to me, albeit in a glib, elliptical, narrative fashion.

Obviously, he was not just the Devil, eternal and unsleeping as he might be, but also *my* Devil. He was a writer's Devil...and, even more specific than that, a science fiction writer's Devil...and, even more specific than that, a quirky science fiction writer's devil, with a distinct pataphysical twist.

Like any hallucination, he was a product of the unconscious mind: both the collective unconscious stocked with the general apparatus of the Cosmic Mind, but my own personal unconscious, warped by my idiosyncratic experiences. The psychotropic produce of Glofeydd Diafol had, however, given him a much greater substance than the normal stuff of my dreams, which were ephemeral, nonsensical and doomed to be soon consigned to oblivion, to an even greater extent than my mortal flesh. As the Devil had said himself, he was not a product of sleep—quite the opposite.

We all know, nowadays, that the matter we can actually see and touch—the matter that lives up to our usual, somewhat deceptive, standards of reality—is only a tiny fraction of the matter that actually exists, most of the substance of the universe consisting of dark matter. We have known for somewhat longer, although we could not initially take advantage of the analogy, that the same is true of the mind: that the fraction of the mind of which consciousness consists, and which therefore seems to us to be "real" in the sense that it is manifest as thought, emotion and reason, is only a tiny fraction of our mentality, most of the directive force of our desires, urges and impulses originating in the dark mind of the unconscious.

In much the same way that physicists have difficulty characterizing dark matter, because our categories of characterization evolved from our understanding of baryonic matter, and hence do not apply to it, psychologists have had difficulty characterizing dark mind, which lies, by definition, beyond consciousness and hence beyond the apparatus that we use to depict and characterize consciousness: the stuff of logic and calculation. It is not easy for reason to get to grips with the irrational.

Perhaps, in the final analysis, it is literally impossible, and we can never obtain any understanding of ourselves beyond the understanding of the tiny, artificial, ephemeral, discontinuous fraction that is our waking, thinking self. But we have resources that can and do help us to achieve insights into the mysteries of the unconscious, because the unconscious does cast shadows, echoes and reflections of various kinds into the conscious mind. Those irruptions can be apprehended, contemplated, and perhaps even partially understood when they take, or can be adapted to, the form of dreams, hallucinations, and, perhaps most important of all, stories.

Stories are the most important way in which the conscious mind tries to adjust and adapt to its juxtaposition with and connection to dark mind. Myths attempt to makes some kind of metaphorical sense of the existence and configuration of the world. Legends attempt to make sense of the relationship between the present and the past. Anecdotes and jokes attempt to take possession of the essential irony and bizarrerie of everyday existence. Fables, parables, apologues, *contes philosophiques* and the entire apparatus of fiction, naturalistic and heterocosmic alike, struggle to grasp and synthesize meanings that make the mere surge of happenstance into an esthetic pattern.

So, I figured, by far and away the most important thing I had to ask myself, regarding the Devil—not merely because of my particular quirky vocation, but because of his very essence, identity and presence—was:

why has he told me that story? Perhaps he would have others to tell me—and, indeed, he had already done so in the guise of various throwaway remarks—but that one, he had not only chosen to tell me at length but had actually prefaced it with the announcement that he was going to tell me a story, and had given it a title. Titles are important, especially when they encapsulate morals.

The ostensible moral of the Devil's story, which he had deliberately stuck out like a hitch-hiker's thumb, was summarized in the dictum that one should never bet he devil your heart, whose meaning was a deliberate antithetical distortion of the previously-proposed dictum that one should never bet the Devil your head. That was what the Devil's story, in essence, had to be trying to tell me. That was what my unconscious mind, the producer and shaper of the hallucination, along with the insistence of the dust of Glofeydd Diafol, was offering me. That had to be the central element of the supposedly-precious knowledge that would constitute his part of the bargain sealed by the pact that is the essence of modern diabolical mythology, in our Faustian Age.

My first thought, as you might well imagine, was that it was an exceedingly meager reward. But then, what did I have to offer him in return? Exactly how much was my soul worth, weighed in the Comic Balance that never lies? The Devil had already told me that he wanted something other than my soul, but I suspected that, even as a mere matter of metaphor and wordplay, my soul was exactly what I had to pledge.

I couldn't help feeling sorry for poor Lucile, though. She had never existed, of course, any more than the Devil did. She was just a narrative device, not a person. The whole story was a tissue of inventions, as all stories are, but that didn't mean that the Devil was lying when he said that he never told lies, because stories, even when they aren't factual, can still be true, in a better, albeit perhaps murkier, sense than mere incidents in the unfolding fabric of happenstance. Tragedy is an aspect of storytelling, and actual events only become tragic when they're narrativized. That's why it makes perfect sense to feel sorry for the characters in fiction, and even to feel greater pity and affection for them even than the actual mortals we admit into the evolving narratives of our waking lives.

So what I actually said to myself, as a result of all the rapid cogitating, all the off-the-cuff philosophizing, and all the desperate seeking for intellectual orientation that I did while the Devil was telling me his story was: "You can try all you like to make yourself out to be a hero, and play the honest man along with the administrator of justice, but the fact remains that you broke that poor girl's heart."

"Precisely," he said.

"And it was an evil thing to do."

"Even if it was, you might care to bear in mind that I'm evil by nature, not by inclination," he reminded me. "I only exist, as a figment of the collective unconscious, specifically to embody the idea of evil, although I've inevitably become confused by the literary representations of the Faustian Age, which have transfigured my image in various sympathetic ways. Fundamentally, though, no matter how hard I try, I just can't get away from the fact that I'm evil. That's why, although there's nothing but good to be gained from wrestling with the idea of me intellectually—betting me your head—there's nothing at all to be gained from taking me on emotionally, metaphorically betting your heart. That way, you'll always lose."

"So, fundamentally," I said, "this hallucination isn't about what I might learn, but about what I can't. When we get right down to it, the only reason you're here is because I'm on my own, nursing a broken heart?"

"If that were the case," the Devil pointed out, "the whole exercise would be a trifle pointless, don't you think? You know as well as I do that self-pity is one of the worst of your many faults, so it might a good idea to try setting it aside and taking advantage of the opportunities provided by our little chat. That coal-dust isn't going to be in your system forever, you know. Eventually, you'll excrete it, just as you piss away everything else in your pointless and pathetic life, so don't you think that it might be as well to try and take advantage of me while I'm here?"

"You're right, obviously," I retorted, slightly stung by the unnecessary insult, "but you'll doubtless forgive me the suspicion that, given that you're a figment of my imagination, you'll ultimately turn out to be just as pointless and pathetic—as you put it—as all the other produce of my imagination. After all, given that you're really just as aspect of myself, even though you do come from the dark part of my mind, beyond the ordinary reach of consciousness, you can't actually tell me anything that I couldn't make up for myself, can you?"

"That is one way to look at it," he conceded, finishing off his glass of wine—which, I now noticed, was the last of the bottle, although I hadn't been aware of refilling the glass, which I had obviously done unconsciously while thinking about other things, "but it's the wrong way. Telling is, in essence, a prerogative of consciousness, an aspect of thinking, so yes, I can't tell you anything that, in principle, you not only could tell yourself but are telling yourself, because I can't think anything that you not only could but are thinking yourself. But it works the other way around, too. You might care to ask yourself whether you're capable of desiring anything that doesn't emerge, fundamentally, from me—which is to say, whether you're capable of manifesting any impulse or direction in your life, any ambition or lust, that doesn't emerge primordially from the unconscious. I'm not just the embodiment of evil, remember, but the embodiment of temptation: the other side of the coin."

I had to admit that he was coming up with arguments I'd never thought of before, even if it was really me that was thinking of them now. But that was my entire life in a nutshell; I was a writer, after all. Of what did my making up stories consist, except bringing to the surface images, ideas and feelings that I'd never glimpsed, conceived or felt before, in order that their creation could assist the processes and development of my mind, perhaps not necessarily improving it, but at the very least assisting in its gradually maturation and metamorphosis, its process of becoming? And wasn't that process a process of discovery, never devoid of surprises?

He was right. What I was doing—or, at least, what I ought to be doing—was betting my head against the Devil. I ought to be confronting my hallucination, if not actually playing poker with him or fighting a duel with rapiers, at least taking him on intellectually. I had to get to grips with him in the way that really mattered, by matching his quips, listening to his stories and trying to make a story out of him, as best I could. Just because he was a figment of my imagination didn't mean that I had nothing to learn from him, nothing to discover in him, no surprises to encounter in supping with him, whether or not I used a long spoon.

"Do you have another bottle?" he asked me, displaying his empty glass.

"I'm not sure that I ought to have any more to drink," I said. "If I get drunk, on top of the Glofeydd Diafol dust, I might become seriously confused—and if I've understood your denial that you had anything to do with the excision of Toby Dammit's head correctly, the only way I can actually lose in betting my head against the Devil is by losing my mind."

"You won't lose your mind," he said. "To lose it, you'd have to find it first. Are you really certain that that's where you're at right now?"

"The possibility that I've already lost it, or never really had it to begin with, has occurred to me," I admitted, "but the fact remains that, given that you're just a figment of my imagination, I'm the only one here who's actually getting drunk, and if I open another bottle, I'm likely to end up with a hell of a hangover."

"You don't have to drink any if you don't want to," the Devil said, "but I need another bottle. As you can see perfectly well, I'm entirely capable of metabolizing it myself, so there's no need to worry about losing control, vomiting or walking up with a hangover…unless, of course you want to, unconsciously."

I went back to the kitchen and got a bottle of cheap *vin de pays*, figuring that it was probably best to be economical in dealing with the Fiend.

When I went back, though, I filled both glasses. It seemed impolite not to join him.

In the meantime, I'd pulled myself together. He was right, and I had to take what advantage I could of his temporary presence. Even if I was, in some sense, talking to myself, that didn't mean that I couldn't learn anything. "Know thyself" is, after all, the first rule of Epicurean philosophy. The second, of course, is "nothing to excess," but you have to take things one at a time.

"So," I said to him, as he looked at me slightly disapprovingly, after taking the first sip from the inferior contents of the second bottle, "what's God like?"

"He isn't *like* anything," he said, "but if you mean, what do I think of him, on the whole, well, he's a trifle annoying. All vanity and vexation of spirit, as the saying goes."

Everybody knows that the Devil can quote scripture, so that wasn't a surprise. "You approve of Ecclesiastes, then?" I observed. "In much wisdom is much grief, and he that increaseth knowledge increaseth sorrow?"

Not exactly an Epicurean sentiment, I reflected.

"I do approve of Ecclesiastes," he confirmed. "Especially in the Tyndall translation. A masterpiece of English poetry, even better than the Hebrew original."

"How about *Genesis*?" I suggested.

"All fabulation, completely lacking in coherency and common sense."

"There never was a Garden of Eden, then?"

"No, of course not."

That was hardly news. "And Jesus?"

"A thoroughly admirable fellow. He should have taken my advice, though."

"When you took him to the top of the high mountain and offered him the kingdoms of the world if he would fall down and worship you?"

"When I paid him a brief visit, assisted by the hallucinatory effects of excessive fasting, and reminded him of what he really already knew but wouldn't admit to himself: that he didn't have to follow that path he was taking to the bitter end, but could settle for the world instead. He could have the ordinary joys of everyday, domestic life, the love of the flesh instead of His love. I didn't promise him happiness, because he knew as well as I do how unreliable human love can be, but I did point out that divine love is even less unreliable, requiring much greater efforts of self-deception. He wouldn't believe me. The faithful never do."

"So you didn't actually offer him the kingdoms of the world?"

"Only in a metaphorical sense, and I didn't demand worship in return for my advice. Worship is His hang-up, not mine."

"I see. What about Faust, then…and all the other tales of pacts and bargaining for souls?"

"Metaphorical, and misunderstood, naturally. Like any storyteller, you know how easy it is for readers, or hearers, to get the wrong end of the stick."

I knew. **** was always trying to construe everything I wrote as an allegory of our marriage, whereas our marriage was actually an allegory of the downbeat conviction of my writing. The more pressing issue, though, was whether or not I could get hold of the right end of the Devil's story-telling stick. It's by no means unknown for writers to misunderstand their own work, especially when they give free rein to the free association of so-called inspiration, and start dredging in the unconscious.

"But there was an actual Faust," I said, "just as there was an actual Jesus?"

"Yes, also an admirable fellow in his way, although far less altruistic. A first-rate scholar, but always something of a substance-abuser, in the academic context of the quest for the doors of perception. I opened them for him, at least by a crack. It wasn't my fault that he didn't like what he saw—he'd read Ecclesiastes, after all, although not in the Tyndall translation. He over-reacted, and started accusing me of cheating—not an uncommon accusation, as you'll remember from my story, but always unjustified, because I always tell the truth. I bluff, but I don't cheat. I didn't have to bargain for his soul, firstly because I didn't want it, secondly because it wasn't worth anything and thirdly because the only damnation to which any soul can be subjected is purely self-inflicted."

"But you did make a pact with him?"

"Oh yes, I did make a pact. Why else would he have summoned me, and why else would I have responded to his summons? It's not as if I don't have other things to do, you know."

"Actually," I confessed, "I'm a trifle confused about that. If there's no Hell, what other things do you have to do, exactly?"

"I supply temptation."

"But why, if you don't get anything out of it?"

"Because it's my *raison d'être*. What I do is determined, inevitably, by what I am. That's another advantage I have over you—I know why I exist; you don't…which is why you have to make up stories to account for it, and also why most of them are so pathetically absurd. It's not your fault, mind—you're made in His image, all vanity and vexation of spirit. You can't help it. It's the human condition."

"But didn't He make you too?"

"Only in a paradoxical sense. I'm His antithesis, so I'm determined by what he's not. If He really were as perfect as He thinks he is, he probably wouldn't need an antithesis, but given the actual quality of Creation, obviously, once you get past the stupid worship thing that demands that you simply assume that He's right *a priori*, it's easy enough to see that there's even more dark matter and dark mind in me than there is in Him. I don't claim to have all the best stories, or all the best tunes, but if you'll forgive the metaphor, I have a hell of a lot of them."

I forgave him the metaphor. There might well be unforgivable sins, but that certainly wasn't one of them.

I backtracked by a few thrusts in the verbal fencing match. "Okay, then," I said, "so you didn't want Faust's soul, and it wasn't worth anything anyway. So what *was* the pact you made with him?"

I was assuming, of course, that it was the same pact he'd come to make with me, although I did have it at the back of my mind that he was probable versatile enough to have more than one pact up his sleeve.

"I already told you, and even the storytellers get that bit right: I opened up the doors of perception by a crack; I gave him a little of the knowledge he craved; I gave him a modicum of enlightenment."

The legend of Faust was formulated at the advent of the Age of Enlightenment; it was, in a sense its Creation myth, its fabular *Genesis*—hence Spengler's characterization of modern era as the Faustian Age.

"I understand that," I told him, wondering if he had genuinely misunderstood my question or whether he was being deliberately obtuse, for the purpose of teasing me. "What I'm curious to know is what he offered you in return—what you got out of the bargain?"

"The only genuine item of value there is in the universe of dark mind, and the authentic substance of the soul: understanding. I'm not a capitalist; I only make honest pacts. I trade understanding for understanding, enlightenment for enlightenment, perception for perception. I helped Faust realize what he needed to know, and he helped me to understand what I need to know. What other kind of trade is possible between the light mind and the dark mind?"

I didn't fail to notice that he was now accusing Faust—and me—of being light-minded, but I had to admit that it was a fair comment, especially as he and I were now half way through the second bottle of wine, and I was beginning to get a trifle light-headed.

"In other words," I said, "Your fundamental motive force is educational? You make pacts with humans in order to find out more about them?"

"You're trivializing it somewhat. It's more complicated than that. Yes, when you look into the abyss, the abyss looks into you, and the learning experience, as well as the esthetic experience, is mutual…but you mustn't leave out the dynamic component."

Light-minded I might have been, by definition, and light-headed I might have been becoming, by virtue of additional substance abuse over and above the devil-dust of the Welsh pit, but I wasn't about to be left behind by the argument. He wasn't talking in riddles; he was just employing the Socratic method, as any good daemon would.

"You're far less mercurial than I am, and far more disciplined in your metamorphoses," I quoted, "but you're not fixed forever. You're eternal, but not unchanging. You evolve. And while you're changing humans, with your temptation, and the perennial challenge of evil, we're changing you—or at least, we have that potential. That's the pact, not just at the personal level of occasional one-to-one encounters, but of the entire Spenglerian era. We're in the process of changing the concept of evil, and hence the nature of evil, in a collective fashion. And you being here, thanks to the dust, is just a tiny fragment of that broader program?"

"That's one way of looking at it," he agreed. "Simplistic, of course, but artificial simplicity is sometimes a useful intellectual strategy, for the light mind. Complication so often leads to confusion."

"And it's different for the dark minded?" I said, skeptically. "No confusion in pandemonium?"

"I can't honestly say that," he answered, as he drained his glass of the dregs of the second bottle of red, "so I won't. On the contrary: the dark mind thrives on paradox, puns and pataphysics—but that doesn't mean that it doesn't have its semblance of order, its deep meanings, and, above all, its esthetics."

There are people in the world who would have challenged his notion that esthetics ranked above all else, but I wasn't one of them. I knew that at the end of the day, even mathematical equations, the laws of physics and the principles of ethics come down to a matter of esthetics. Truth is beauty and beauty truth, and although that certainly isn't all that we need to know, it's the foundation stone of the edifice.

"So, by way of summation," I said, "you're here in order that you and I can make a pact. You'll enlighten me if I enlighten you. You've already answered a lot of my questions, I admit—so what is it you that want to ask me?"

"Well," he said, "since you...."

That, unfortunately, was the point at which I threw up—after which my head began to spin, everything went dark and I probably lost consciousness. At least, I couldn't remember anything more until the following day, and still can't, the rest being lost in the darkness of the mind.

CHAPTER X

If ever the Devil tells you that it's safe to drink with him because you won't throw up and won't get a hangover, don't believe him.

I wish that weren't true, because I really would have liked to believe his assurance that he never tells lies, but in my experience, at least, he is not a person to be trusted completely, and once trust has gone, once one simple lie, however trivial, has exposed the falsity of the universal generalization, then you can never be sure of anything that a person tell you is true.

Actually, you never can anyway. Even if you never catch someone out in a lie, you simply cannot believe anyone's assertion that they always tell the truth. There is no such thing as perfect reliability, even on the part of Him—especially, in fact, on the part of Him. It is literally true that no one is or can be perfect. No matter how spotless their record to date might be, the possibility always exists that the next affirmation might be a downright lie.

The Devil might have tried to counter an accusation that he had lied about the vomiting and the hangover by reminding me that he'd only said that I wouldn't suffer those things unless I wanted to unconsciously—but that's an essentially dishonest strategy, and an unfalsifiable assertion, because it always leaves you the option of arguing that whatever happened is what you wanted to happen, unconsciously.

With all due respect to Eric Berne, I did *not* want that hangover. Depressed I certainly was, but certainly not determined to punish myself for my sins in such a futile and underhanded fashion.

So, to get back to the story, I woke up on Wednesday morning with one hell of a hangover, at least sufficient to suggest to me that even though there were two used glasses on the coffee table, I really had drunk the whole two bottles myself, and felt the entirety of their metabolic effects myself. Doubtless, if that had been the case—or even if it hadn't, and the Devil really had taken his fair share of intoxication away with him—the effects of the dust of Glofeydd Diafol had added their component to the synergistic mix.

I had, of course, had a sleepless night the night before, and I was suffering from some kind of insidious poisoning as well as the effects of the alcohol, so it's not particularly astonishing that I had slept unusually heavily and for an unusually long time, but I was still rather surprised to find, when I woke up—still fully dressed and lying on the sofa—that it was half past eleven.

By the time I'd scrubbed the vomit out of the carpet, as best I could, and drunk half a pint of water and two cups of black coffee, taken three paracetamol and had a bowl of Weetabix, it was way past noon and half the day was gone, utterly wasted without a shot being fired against the besieging forces of writer's block.

I wasn't feeling much like working anyway. I had a terrible hangover, and once the paracetamol took effect and the headache gradually began to ease, I needed to think. I had, after all, met the Devil, and had spent what must have been getting on for two or three hours in earnest discussion with him regarding the terms of a possible pact. That's not the kind of thing that happens every day, and it is definitely the sort of thing that requires a certain amount of investigation after the fact.

Inevitably, such inquests begin with the question: "Am I going mad?" and continue with the supplementary interrogation: "Have I already gone mad?" but anyone with an atom of common sense doesn't waste time lingering over such trivial queries. There were far more important things about which to wonder than mere issues of sanity.

For one thing, of course, I felt guilty, as one would after a close encounter with the Devil, especially one that had not involved a long spoon. I felt guilty because I feared that I might have short-changed him. One way or another, he really had given me a lot of information, which probably did qualify as enlightenment even if, in the light of the hangover issue, his dogged assertion of his own truthfulness had to be regarded as a trifle dubious. On the other hand, as soon as he had begun to formulate a question that might have permitted me to reciprocate, in my doubtless modest and light minded fashion, I had conked out.

I had failed to keep my part of the bargain.

I knew, of course, having read a lot of deal-with-the-devil stories, that most writers consider cheating in the context of diabolical pacts to be not merely permissible but *de rigueur*. I have never considered that to be ethical, however—or, more importantly, esthetic. If you make a pact with the Devil, it seems to me, you are honor bound to keep it. If you have promised him your soul, you ought to deliver. What kind of person does it make you if you welsh on the deal? Worse than him, at a minimum, if he has followed through with his part and supplied the things you demanded. If you have voluntarily offered yourself for damnation, in return for various concessions, then you should damned well *be* damned, or else—however paradoxically—you are simply proving that you are damnable.

I did not want to be found wanting in my own dealings with the Devil, but I could not be certain, that Wednesday afternoon, that I would have a chance to make good. After all, if the effects of the dust of Glofeydd Diafol were to wear off during the day, I might not see him again, and if Martin followed through with his threat to burn the books and mount a full-scale assault with the vacuum cleaner, I would very probably not have the opportunity to repeat the experiment.

It did occur to me that I would still have the option of going to Pwllmerys itself; even though the pit itself had presumably been sealed when the old National Coal Board of 1947-1987 had closed it down, there still had to be a lot of dust from its special brand of coal lying around in the vicinity. On the other hand, I had a suspicion that mere superficial dirt wouldn't do the job, or heaps of slag. The dust I'd imbibed, as I'd already observed, had been incubating in the boxes in which the remnants of the library had been stored for a long time, and it wasn't just dust, it was book-dust. The coal-dust had been mingled, not merely with tangible paper-dust and ink-dust, but the dark-matter dust of intellect and rhetoric, and even though the books in question had been tedious, at least from my point of view, they were nevertheless products of human intellectual and esthetic endeavor, which someone had taken the effort to write, under the spur of the urge to communicate and persuade, to impress and exhibit.

I couldn't help wondering what the dust might have produced if only the books had been better books, if only the spirit of Émile de Girardin's Romanticism hadn't been squeezed out of them by a much duller and more pedantic notion of education. If the library really had consisted, as it surely should have done, of the works of Lord Byron and Percy Shelley, William Blake and Thomas Love Peacock, Thomas Spence and Mary Wollstone-craft, what a Devil they might have produced in association with the fuel of Glofeydd Diafol!

Not that I was complaining about my Devil, of course, but not all Devils are equal. Some are more evil than others, some more tempting, and some—but not, I fear, mine, let alone that of the Welsh Chapel—blessed with genius.

At any rate, I had no guarantee, that Wednesday afternoon, that the Devil would return, so that I could make good on my promise, and, as I say, I felt guilty about that, as an honest man would.

I tried to console myself with the thought that if the Devil really wanted to come back, he would surely be able to do so, perhaps even without the assistance of the magic coal-dust, if, in fact I had pissed that away. After all, we were acquainted now, and he no longer had to observe the same polite protocol. I hadn't actually told him, in so many words, to drop in any time, but I think it had probably been tacitly understood, even though the fact that I'd deliberately opened an inferior bottle of wine after we'd finished the first was a sin against the principles of hospitality.

It was while I was trying hard to assure myself that the Devil could drop in again if he wanted to, even if he only had the natural resources of my dark mind to draw upon henceforth, that another thought struck me, which disturbed me slightly, although there was no logical reason why it should.

What if the Devil didn't need to come back? What if he didn't need to talk to me again in order that I could fulfill my part of the bargain we'd tacitly struck? What if I'd already fulfilled my part of the bargain, *unconsciously*?

After all, I couldn't be entirely certain that I had stopped talking when the last chapter cut off. I couldn't remember having said another word, but that didn't necessarily mean that I hadn't, and even if I hadn't said another word, that didn't necessarily mean that my mind hadn't continued working, in a fashion that Devil could read and comprehend. He was, after all, an inhabitant of the dark mind…and more precisely than that, of *my* dark mind.

Perhaps he could have obtained what he wanted without my even knowing it. It would have been sneaky, and perhaps a trifle unfair, but in spite of the revisionist reinterpretation he'd offered of himself, he did have a reputation….

I refused to believe it, of course. I decided that, in spite of the slip with regard to the vomiting and the hangover, I would continue to trust him, at least for a little while longer. I decided that he *would* come back, if he could, and that he would give me the chance to answer his questions in the light of mind, consciously, conscientiously and judiciously, as befitted a decent human being and a half-way decent science fiction writer.

In the meantime, though, I decided that in order to do that, I needed to give a little more thought to the answers that I was going to give, in order that they would, in fact, be as conscientious and judicious as I could contrive.

I was slightly handicapped by the fact that I didn't know exactly what questions he might ask, but that was only a quibble. All I had to do was ask myself what the Devil would, in fact need to know in order to continue and facilitate the metamorphosis of the collective unconscious, at least within my own dark mind and perhaps more generally.

That seemed simple enough, and I had the Devil's own word for it that simplicity is sometimes a useful intellectual strategy.

So what did the collective unconscious need to know, if its hypothetical archetypes were to work progressively on the task of their own self-improvement?

It was a good question—or so it seemed at the time.

I took three more paracetamol, drank half a liter or orange juice and made myself two fried eggs on two slices of fried wholemeal bread before trying to get to grips with it, and I also ate a Mars bar in order to boost my sugar supply. I felt better after that, although I knew I wouldn't be winning any awards for healthy eating and a balanced diet.

Then I started thinking, very seriously, albeit simplistically—for tactical reasons—about the nature of the unconscious, the dark mind that supplies the greater component of human mentality.

I began, logically enough, at the beginning, with Schopenhauer, or what I could remember of his argument without actually looking it up—you will remember that it was 1997 and that Wikipedia did not yet exist, so "looking up" still involved a certain amount of heavy physical labor.

Put bluntly, I reminded myself, Schopenhauer's argument was that life, liberty and the pursuit of happiness is a bad bet, which no rational student of probability would take on. Even the most cursory study of the operation of the world suffices to demonstrate that the sum of pleasure therein is far less than the sum of pain, and that the raw probability of getting through life with a tolerable minimum of pain and a satisfactory dose of pleasure is a lot less than evens. In terms of the calculus of probability, the game is not worth the candle. That's where the dark mind comes in: by supplying us with an unconscious "will to survive" that drives us on against the odds, taking the conscious form of such blatantly deceptive but perhaps psychologically necessary illusions as hope, faith and optimism. In spite of the odds, and even in spite of knowing the odds, we keep on thinking that things might work out anyway.

The unconscious will to survive isn't limited in its behavioral expressions and conscious refractions to mere matters of self-preservation, of course, but has corollaries in terms of urges to ambition and competition—which is to say, to the enhancement of one's own survival chances at the expense of others—and also urges to indulge in behaviors favorable to successful reproduction, including sex and parental care. All its conscious manifestations are, of course, subject to various degrees of corruption and perversion as well as varying degrees of intensity, which are collectively responsible for the majority of individual character traits.

There are also, according to Schopenhauer and others, various ways in which the conscious mind can attempt to compensate for the natural stacking of the odds against the likelihood of avoiding pain and maximizing pleasure, a few of which actually work, to some degree, although many simply engage in an ultimately hopeless struggle to beat the odds by means of ingenuity, self-deception and enhanced perversity.

Naturally, psychologists have attempted all manner of sophistications of that basic template, by means of descriptive observation and prescriptive recommendation, attempting much more elaborate analyses of the hypothetical contents and mechanisms of the dark mind, and more elaborate prescriptions for the assistance of consciousness in its attempts to supplement or substitute for the blind and crude urges supplied by the unconscious. Most such frills, however, are fantasies of one kind or another, whose successes depend almost entirely on the placebo effect.

Attempts to investigate the workings of the dark mind via electrical analysis of brain activity rather than by introspection—or, as in Axel Castle's experiment, in which I'd volunteered to help out the following week, by a combination of the two—have complicated understanding further in some interesting ways, but haven't yet added very much to traditional forms of "mindbending" or "brainwashing" techniques intended to give outsiders a measure of control over the dark and light minds of others.

Where did the Devil fit into all that? Well, I supposed, in terms of Jungian jargon, he was an archetype of the collective unconscious: a particular parcel of urges, the psychological and behavioral effects of which consciousness has little option but to characterize, and has a strong temptation to personalize. He was an idea, formed in antithesis to and close association with the idea of a divine Creator responsible for existence and organization, routinely characterized and often personalized, as the Cosmic Mind, if not simply as God.

The Devil I had actually talked to was not the archetype itself, of course, but merely a conscious image thereof, a reflection adapted to consciousness—both generally and idiosyncratically—by the imagination. Other people fortunate enough to meet him would doubtless have seen him differently and would have had a very different conversation, even though he would have been fundamentally the same and the one and only Devil, and many of those other seers would not have had the delusion, no matter how much of the dust of Glofeydd Diafol or some biochemical equivalent they had absorbed, that he had offered them the kind of pact that he had offered me.

Many people, in fact, believe that the collective component of the dark mind is essentially unchangeable, and that it is only the personal and idiosyncratic modifications made to it by various kinds of mindbending, operating via consciousness, that remain amenable to modification or repair, by means of the same processes. Such people believe that even dealing with personal neuroses is difficult, although not hopeless, but that attempting to deal with the neuroses of the entire race—the innate and hereditary components of the collective unconscious—is beyond the scope of individual action, even within the arena of the individual brain and mind, let alone on any larger scale.

Clearly, I didn't believe that, or I would never have conceived of the Devil as I had conceived him. At the very least, I had to believe in the theoretical possibility that making a formal pact with the Devil, provided that we each lived up fully to our end of it, might enable me to bring about some modification in the archetypal architecture of my own unconscious—and perhaps, given the right environmental circumstances, enable me to persuade at least a few other people that similar modifications were possible and desirable.

Evidently, I had to believe in the latter possibility too, because I was a writer, and what can the *raison d'être* of a writer possibly be except to communicate his ideas to other people and influence, more or less ingeniously, the way they think? Even the most unsuccessful writer in the world—and I was not so very far off that status in 1997, although I am considerably closer to it now—has to nurse that ambition, even if bitter experience shows him how heavily the odds are stacked against him, and even if his stocks of faith, hope and optimism stand so close to zero as to be equivalent to frank despair. Even if all he that has going for him is simple pig-headed Yorkshire obstinacy, he cannot and does not give up, especially when, at least once in his life, he has encountered the Devil and sworn to uphold the pact that he has made with him.

So, on that Wednesday, albeit somewhat numb and enfeebled in my intellectual acuity because of the after-effects of the dust of Glofeydd Diafol, the hangover and the paracetamol, I knew that my time had come to attempt to be a hero, even if I only were only to end up an absurd Don Quixote, and that I had to figure out what I was going to tell the Devil, if and when I saw him again, and if and when he took up the questioning where my sudden attack of nausea had presumably forced him to break off.

In order to facilitate that task I decided to walk to Asda, partly because I had run out of bread, eggs and various other vital food supplies, and partly because I thought it might be wise to stock up on cheap wine, just in case the Devil was going to make further demands on my hospitality. I wanted to save the last bottle of Pinot Noir from Boulogne for a possible celebration, if **** ran true to form and decided to come back again, at least for a while.

As it happens, she eventually did—ten more times in the course of a further decade, in fact—before she finally vanished forever into the toils of divorce, but that would be another story, and one that will remain forever untold, because it is essentially devoid of interest, significance and incapable of any possible influence on the dark or light mind of anyone.

Asda was a mile and a half away from home, mostly along the aptly-named Wilderness Road, so it took approximately half an hour to walk there and slightly longer to walk back carrying a rucksack full of supplies. I knew every step of the way by heart so I could do it on automatic pilot, and I always found it a useful opportunity for cogitation and for doing the kind of work that writers have to do when they are not actually tapping keys—the sort of work that no writer's spouse will ever believe that he or she is doing, that it needs doing, or even that it can be done, which is why the divorce rate among writers is so much higher than average.

But I digress. On that Wednesday, I devoted the half hour spent walking to Asda and the half hour return journey to thinking about what I was going to tell the Devil, if he condescended to return that night, in order to fulfill my part of the pact. I knew that the only benefit I was likely to get out of it, if any benefit were possible at all, was personal—that the only person on whose dark mind I had any real chance of having even the slightest influence was my own—but I didn't want to go into the situation in that frame of mind. I wanted to think like a writer, of constructing arguments that might have some kind of rhetorical or persuasive force, provided that they were cast in an appropriate form.

What I mean by an *appropriate* form is, essentially, an *elliptical* form. The truth requires its own rhetoric, far more than lies, because the truth, unlike lies, doesn't have its own persuasiveness already built in. Lies are intended to persuade and deceive, and are designed from scratch with that purpose. The truth isn't designed to persuade—because the truth simply *is*, and is therefore designed by the Cosmic Mind, simply *to be*. It has to be discovered, and when it is, it often turns out to be difficult, frequently absurd and usually not very persuasive at all, on the surface.

The best way, and perhaps the only way, to make the truth palatable, let alone persuasive, is to formulate it as fiction, as fable, parable, comedy, satire or tragedy. Not all writers want to tell the truth, of course, and those who only want to tell people what they want to hear—which is, let's face it, the only way to appeal to a lot of readers—are usually liars, but even they usually have sufficient conscience to want to slip a little truth in there surreptitiously, because they are, after all, writers, and would have chosen to do something else if they did not have that *raison d'être*.

So, while trying to work out what answer to give the Devil if and when our conversation resumed and our pact was completed, I was already thinking of various ways that it might be cast in fictional form, and made into a story—not the one you are reading at present, obviously, as I knew full well that no one in 1997 would ever condescend to publish this one. I knew that I would have to wait for a new era of small press publication to become economically viable, or for self-publication to become much easier, if it were ever to be worth the effort of telling it like it actually was rather than simply reproducing the bare bones of the tale of the haunted bookshop as a kind of quirky joke.

"The most important thing of all," I said to the imaginary Devil by way of rehearsal of what I might say to the one who, although non-existent, was nevertheless real and material, "is to undermine the supposed certainties of the dark mind. The most vital thing is to adopt a strategy of opposition to the obvious. Whatever seems to be unassailable needs to be challenged. Only by first weakening the existing supportive structures of the dark mind can it be prepared for evolution and metamorphosis. Cynicism is vital; without the spread of cynicism, as widely and as deeply as possible, no progress is even conceivable. Wherever there is certainty, we must sow doubt, and wherever there is optimism, we must sow fear. Otherwise, we'll simply be stuck in the conservative mind—which, believe me, does not have the redemptive potential of the dust of Glofeydd Diafol.

"We must pay attention not merely to the content of the stories that we tell and try spread but also to the form and narrative strategy. The deadliest of all diseases of fiction is the standard story-arc that concludes a story by reversing or compensating for some distortion introduced in the course of the plot by means of an apparent return to normality—what the technical jargon calls a 'happy ending.' The first duty of a serious writer, and hence of a serious Devil, is to undermine the mythology of the 'happy ending,' to defeat and defy the feelgood factor that slyly suggests to readers that they ought to feel joyful if things are returned to 'normal,' and to assert instead that only a transformation and transcendence of normality can really qualify as a satisfactory or interesting conclusion.

"The endings of stories, and hence the stories themselves, ought to suggest insistently and repetitively, and should assert as cleverly as humanly possible, that consciousness should never be so light-minded as to be satisfied with normality, that it should always be striving for something different, because there is no other way of exploring the possibility of something better. There is nothing wrong with levity, which is inherently opposed to gravity, but light minds should be buoyant, not insubstantial, and they should never be *content*.

"That ought to become the basic strategy of future temptation, the first objective of future mischief. It is, by definition, the Devil's work, and the writer's duty, and it is the manner in which you and I ought to work in collaboration, in future."

I stopped there, not because I couldn't go on—believe me I can go on and on and on—but because it pays to keep things simple, and take things one step at a time. Enlightenment is an intrinsically slow process, and more haste sometimes leads to less speed, or even to overheating and breakdown.

In any case, I had reached home again, and my headache had come back in no uncertain manner. I was in dire need of three paracetamol and a lie down before dinner.

CHAPTER XI

I didn't actually get as far as the bed before the telephone rang. I was strongly tempted to let it ring until the answerphone condescended to take it, but the ringtone seemed particularly grating, so I picked it up.

"Hello," I said.

"Mr. Stableford?"

"Yes," I said, warily. The age of nuisance callers had already begun, even though it hadn't reached the plague proportions it has attained today.

"It's Penny, from the SPR. We met on Monday, for the vigil at Martin's bookshop, and we both volunteered for the experiment at the university next week."

"Indeed," I said, surprised. "What can I do for you?"

"I'm sorry if I'm disturbing you, but I wanted to ask you whether you were feeling okay. I think you were right, you see, about there being something in the bookshop that might make us ill. I seemed to be all right once I got back into the fresh air, but...."

For a moment, I actually thought she was going to say that she had met the Devil—but that, of course, was absurd. If she had, there was absolutely no way that she would say so, especially to me.

"Well," she continued, after a slight pause, her Welsh accent coming out more strongly as embarrassment took hold, "the long and the short of it is that I'm not feeing too clever today, and I've seen Martin, who looks distinctly the worse for wear. I phoned Lionel, but he's his usual self—nothing gets him down—but I thought...just to complete the picture...I ought to see how you are."

"Actually," I confessed, "I've got a terrible headache. It's partly my own fault—I had a drink last night, trying to dispel a vague feeling of being under the weather, and I think that made things worse. I don't think it's anything serious, though. It could be a virus, or it could be fungal spores or something else I breathed in while we were in the shop, but I'm sure it will pass."

Unlike the Devil, I lie all the time.

"Right," she said. "I thought, being a biologist, that you might have some idea of what it is...given that, as there are three of us feeling under the weather, it's probably not psychosomatic."

"I can't offer any specific hypothesis, I'm afraid," I told her, "but as I say, I don't think the symptoms are serious, and it will probably pass...as least so far as you and I are concerned, and probably Martin too."

"Okay," she said. "I'll see how I feel tomorrow. Claire Louchon dropped round, but she doesn't seem worried either."

It took me a few seconds to realize that Claire Louchon must be Axel Castle's collaborator. "Oh, no," I said, "I'm sure it will have cleared up be next week. I'm coming to Pontypridd on Tuesday, but I assume I won't see you there, as they can only do one volunteer at a time."

"That's right," she said. "You're before me, then—my first session is set for Thursday. It sounds interesting, although I must confess that I can't actually believe that it's really going to put us in telepathic contact with the Cosmic Mind."

"I don't think telepathy is what they're aiming at," I observed. "It's more a matter of trying to stimulate neural connections inducing an alternative state of consciousness—something akin to nirvana. The reference to the Cosmic Mind is just a metaphor, so far as I can judge from what Axel told me."

"Right," she said. "Claire was a bit vague. She didn't want to put ideas into my head, she said, in case it prejudiced my expectations. She muttered something about Heisenberg's Uncertainty Principle, but I think she just meant the act of observation influencing the properties of the observed— the curse of psychological and sociological research, as they used to say at the LSE."

"I used to say the same when I was teaching at Reading," I told her. "Personally, I think that referencing the Cosmic Mind is a blunder on Axel's part. He should have made up some opaque jargon that would just sound like gobbledygook to the guinea-pigs. Not that suggestive prejudice of that sort will affect me, of course."

"Of course not," she said, sounding less than entirely convinced. "Well, even if I don't see you, good luck with it."

"Thanks," I said. It seemed only polite.

"Bye," she said, and rang off.

I was intrigued by the call—not so much by anything she'd said as because she'd made it. It would have been easy enough for her to get my number from Lionel if she'd spoken to him, so she hadn't gone to any real trouble, but she must actually be more worried about her condition than she had let on, and if, as she suggested, Martin had had something of a relapse, perhaps while trying to tidy up after me in the upstairs room, then the book-shop might indeed by measurably toxic, albeit not literally haunted.

I was almost tempted to ring Martin myself, to find out more about what he'd been doing in the shop and exactly what the effects were. I knew, though, that if he had seen any kind of hallucination, the chances of his spelling out the details to me were very thin…although he might spell them out to Lionel if he went back to the idea of a precautionary exorcism.

I decided, on reflection, that it could probably wait until next week, when Lionel, who would doubtless keep up to date with the situation, could fill me in one the remainder of the story.

I did have a nap thereafter, and I ate dinner late again, as I had on the previous night. I felt considerably better afterwards, so the nap had obviously helped. Once again, thanks to the summer schedule, there was nothing on TV that I wanted to watch, so, when I'd washed up, I went back into the front room intending to pick up my neglected book.

Once again, I had hardly begun to reach for it when I became aware of the Devil sitting in the same armchair, in the same relaxed attitude, wearing the same red cravat.

"I wasn't sure that I'd see you again," I said.

"I wasn't sure that I'd see you," he countered, "but here we are."

"It's very kind of you," I said, "considering all the things you must have to do, to pay so much heed to a soul as mediocre as mine."

"You don't mean that," he observed, accurately, in a neutral tone.

"Sorry," I said, insincerely. "I've been thinking hard all day, though, about the way to conclude our pact, and I think I've worked out an argument that might satisfy its terms."

"I know," he said, "I've been listening in on your thoughts from the shadows of your mind. To be perfectly honest, though, I know all of that pseudointellectual bullshit already, and I'd really rather you didn't bother with any of it. I know that you're a writer, but without meaning to be insulting, even humble creators of that petty sort do have a tendency to be a little too self-involved and intellectually self-indulgent, which I find rather trying, vanity- and vexation-wise. That isn't what I wanted to ask you about at all, as you'd have discovered if you hadn't started throwing up all over the place. Could you possibly open one of the bottles you bought at Asda, by the way? I won't be so impolite as to ask you to open the Pinot Noir that you want to save, even though you won't be needing it for a couple of months."

"Are you saying now that you *can* foretell the future?" I asked.

"No, but I'm a good judge of probabilities. I also know that you bought the wine in case I came back, even though you know perfectly well that it's not my favorite tipple, so you can't have any rational objection to opening it."

"You won't mind if I don't join you, though. I need a sober evening."

"I won't mind at all," he assured me, perhaps with the ghost of a smile.

I opened a bottle, but only brought one glass, just to make sure that I avoided temptation—at least to the extent that such avoidance might be possible while negotiating with the Devil.

I filled the glass for him, and then abandoned the bottle to his own devices. It was Australian Shiraz, perfectly drinkable but a little more full-bodied than the wines I usually preferred.

"Well," I said to him, "if you aren't interested in my theories regarding the progressive education of the unconscious, what were you about to ask me when malaise intervened?"

"I was about to ask you what you think I ought to have done about Lucile?"

The extent to which one can be caught by surprise by a figment of one's own imagination is really quite surprising.

"Lucile?" I echoed, taken aback.

"The young woman in the story that I told you about," he reminded me. "The one who became infatuated with me, effectively betting her heart on me."

"I don't know," I said. "That's not a problem I've ever had to deal with."

"It is now," he said. "Hypothetically, at least. What should I have done? I did tell her the truth, remember. I didn't make any false promises. Should I have rejected her when I left the house, do you think, on the grounds that breaking her heart then would be somehow kinder than breaking it later?"

"You could have refrained from breaking it at all," I pointed out.

"Not forever," he pointed out, "or even for her lifetime. I could only refrain in the short term, in fact, by maintaining a pretence that was becoming increasingly burdensome as well as transparent, and which would soon have been obvious not merely to her but to everyone else, given my essential honesty. Do you really think that there was any way that she could have been preserved for very long from catastrophic disappointment?"

"Perhaps not," I admitted, warily.

"I'm not saying that it wasn't my fault, of course," the Devil, "although you might well have attempted denial, if you ever had been in my position. Unfortunately, as the personification of temptation, I can hardly deny responsibility for the fact that she was tempted, into a situation that had no exit."

"It's a puzzle," I admitted. "I'm afraid that I don't have an answer. Personally, on the rare occasions that I write love stories, they tend to end tragically or perversely, but you already know all about my manifesto for the abolition of happy endings. It's not what I once hoped for in real life, of course, but that's merely a reflection of the extent to which the odds are stacked in the configuration of reality. I'm older and wiser now."

He didn't seem to want to discuss Schopenhauerian philosophy, even though the extent of my acquired wisdom was supposedly the whole point of our conversation, and the substance of our pact. I was disappointed, although admittedly not disastrously so.

"What about Jesus?" he asked.

"What about Jesus?" I riposted, again taken by surprise.

"Do you think that I gave him the right advice in suggesting that he ought to settle for the world, and life, and everyday compensations, instead of pursuing his supposedly divine mission?"

I was very tempted to reply that, given my estimation of the manner in which the odds are stacked against the likelihood that the compensations of everyday life would have delivered anything resembling happiness, it probably wouldn't have mattered much, but that would have been unfair, as even a bad marriage can only lead to metaphorical crucifixion—believe me, I know—and literal crucifixion is definitely several orders of magnitude worse. So I answered the question seriously, once I'd given it a few moments' thought.

"I think you were right," I said. "I know there's an argument that the example set by Christ's crucifixion eventually did a lot of good by providing a lot of people with consolations, but the Church hasn't been an unalloyed blessing. I know that there have always have been lots of people in it like Lionel, whose hearts are in the right place and who really do help out their fellows, but you have to balance that against the crusades, the Inquisition, and the patent fact that the whole enterprise is a betrayal and travesty of his ideas, given that he was really an individualistic anarchist. So yes, I think you were right, that Jesus would have benefited himself, and that the world probably wouldn't be a worse place if he had taken your advice."

"But you wouldn't generalize the advice, would you?" he queried. "You wouldn't want to advise *everyone* to settle for the world as it is, and the compensations that it offers, because that would run directly contrary to the principle that you formulated so proudly while you were walking back from the supermarket?"

"Touché," I admitted.

"And given that I can't foretell the future, and thus had no inkling of the fact that Jesus was going to get himself crucified, let alone that his followers were going to form a Church that would, in your opinion, betray and travesty all his principles, what you ought to think, if you want to be self-consistent, is that, given the limited information I had, I shouldn't have given him that advice at all."

He had me there. Honesty compelled me to admit it." I suppose so," I said, grudgingly.

"What about Faust?" he added, relentlessly. "Given that I've explained the pact that I actually made with him, rather than the one credited by lurid legend, do you think it was a fair deal?"

I was warier by now, but even so I said: "It seems to me that he got what he wanted: enlightenment, and it certainly doesn't seem to me that he paid too high a price for it. If it's the same deal that you're offering me, then I'll certainly take it, and if Spengler's right, the entire modern era already has taken it, tacitly, except for a few stick-in-the-muds."

"Even though I believe that in much wisdom is much grief, and he that increaseth knowledge increaseth sorrow?" he reminded me.

I didn't have to ask him why, if that was what he thought, he had offered Faust enlightenment. He was, after all, evil incarnate.

Instead, I stuck up for him: "I still think it was a good deal," I said. "Enlightenment—knowledge and wisdom, that is—is precious. It's worth paying the price, even in a modicum of grief and sorrow. The poison is the dose, after all, and without knowing grief and sorrow, how would we be able to measure the value of the rare moments of satisfaction that we do succeed in acquiring—more often by means of enlightenment, in my view, than ignorance, whatever people might say about its blissful nature."

He nodded, as if making a concession. "Thank you for that," he said. "I appreciate the sympathy."

I couldn't see that it was helping much, even in the education of my own dark mind, let alone the vaster reaches of the collective unconscious, but it seemed impolite to say so.

"I can't see the future, of course," he said, "so I don't know what's likely to happen next week, but you'll forgive me if I take your assertion of your skeptical immunity to any kind of suggestion with a pinch of salt, given that you're perfectly willing to chat on friendly terms with the Devil. So let me ask you, hypothetically, what you're going to say next Tuesday or Wednesday, if Alex Castle's computerized method of hypnosis really does manage to put you in touch with Him?"

I hadn't actually thought about it, and admitted as much. "Why?" I asked him. "Is there something you'd like me to the Cosmic Mind, if I do get in touch with it—Him, that is?"

"Well, obviously," he said, "given that I'm His antithesis—but I know from experience that it's not as easy to deny Him when you're actually looking into the Countenance Divine as it is when you have your back turned. Not that I'm taking it for granted that the experiment's going to work, of course—its been tried before and failed, but with computer power increasing exponentially, and measuring devices for tracking what's going in inside the brain becoming more sophisticated all the time, the dark mind really is going to become increasingly accessible to the probing of consciousness, and it might be only a matter of time before its archetypes are laid bare. I don't mind personally, of course…but I wouldn't be entirely surprised if there were…disappointments."

"Disastrous disappointments?"

"Perhaps."

"For whom?"

"Difficult to tell—but the potential is there."

"For me?"

"I don't know."

"But you think I ought to think about it?"

"Don't you?"

"Is this part of our pact?"

"Oh, no—that's just between us, and I'm perfectly satisfied with my part of that bargain."

"In spite of the mediocrity of my soul and the fact that you think the enlightenment I hoped to offer you is just pseudointellectual bullshit?"

"That's not your fault. You can only bargain with what you have, and can only provide the enlightenment you can provide."

"Perhaps you ought to be grateful for its mediocrity, then—less wisdom and less knowledge, less grief and less sorrow."

"I don't feel grief or sorrow. I'm the Devil. That's why the bargain isn't really fair. You're the only one at risk."

I looked at him hard, wondering whether I could believe him. I had, after all, exposed his unreliability. Could I really believe that he didn't feel grief or sorrow, even if he was the Devil…especially if he was the Devil? He certainly seemed to regret Lucile, even though circumstance had left him no alternative but to break her heart. In a way, I suppose, I had cause to be grateful that circumstance had never forced me to break anyone's heart, even though it was difficult to feel the gratitude in question, because it really would have been nice, in a prideful sort of way, to think that I might have the capacity to induce someone to love me.

But I realized that I was looking at the question the wrong way, that I had fallen victim to a logical error. The Devil was a creature of the dark mind, of the source of the urges of which the emotions are the conscious manifestations. Of course he couldn't feel emotions himself; that would have been a contradiction in terms, and no matter how generous the physical universe might be in admitting paradoxes, there was no way of escaping the inevitability of that one. Emotions belong to the light mind, no matter how dark-edged they sometimes appear to be; the archetypes of the unconscious, even if we sometimes make the imaginative effort to personalize then, to give them images and names, and put flesh on them in order that they can visit us and converse with us and make pacts with us, are entities that cannot possibly feel grief or sorrow, love or hate, joy or misery. They are the source of all those things, but the things themselves are refractions and shadows, intrinsically and essentially estranged from their source.

The Devil could not feel grief or sorrow. So why, I wondered, was he asking me questions about how he should have handled the Lucile problem, or what advice he ought to have given Jesus, or whether he had really done Faust a favor, or what I might say if, by some freak of neurological circumstance, Axel Castle's experiment really did put me in contact with the Cosmic Mind—which could not really be a "Him" even to the extent that the Devil, with a little help from me, could be?

Why was he asking me such questions, and trying to strike a bargain, that could not possibly be meaningful to him—to the Devil behind and within the disguise with which my imagination had obligingly clothed him?

He'd told me himself, of course, in his own truthful fashion—the fashion of telling the truth in such a way that it would be misunderstood, misinterpreted, or simply missed.

He was in search of enlightenment: an impossible enlightenment, which would be forever beyond his grasp, because he was essentially an aspect of, and eternally confined by, dark mind, but about which he could not help but gravitate.

I—which is to say, my light mentality, my feelings, my soul—was the Devil's pornography, stimulating something within him that was not lust, because he could no more feel lust than he could experience love or sorrow, but which somehow substituted for it in the pattern of his being, within the metaphorical black hole that he was, beyond the event horizon of the light mind.

And I suddenly wondered why, given the dimensions of freedom that I had in conferring an image and solidity upon him, in making him matter in the sense of being the possibility of sensation, I had given him that red cravat.

No sooner had I formulated the question, inevitably, than I knew the answer.

Baudelaire, when he had made the sartorial decision that henceforth, "his only colors would be black," had made the exception that he would wear a red cravat, because it would give the impression that he had been freshly guillotined, that he was walking around with his head cut off, impelled not by life but some strange afterlife: that he was, in effect, a kind of ghoul.

People thought, of course, that he was just making a macabre joke, typical of his perverse sense of humor, but he was a writer, and all his truest remarks were made in a spirit of diabolical bluff, so that no one could or would believe them. I had always suspected that the poor fellow really did feel as if he were walking around with his head cut off, at least metaphorically and symbolically, and as if he really were a kind of ghoul.

Baudelaire's biographers, I knew, had always struggled to understand his fatal and baneful relationship with his mistress, Jeanne Duval, who treated him appallingly and continually left him, but whom he always let back in when she turned up on his doorstep. Most of them, being mere biographers, attempting to understand him from a clinical point of view, without a proper sense of esthetics, had tended to assume that it was a matter of some kind of indomitable passion, some kind of perverse but ineradicable love, but I felt—because I thought about it as a writer would, admittedly one with a very mediocre soul—that I understood him more fully than that, and more intimately.

I thought that the reason the Baudelaire had always let Jeanne Duval back into his life, even though he knew that she was a toxic presence, was because she was better than nothing, and because, without her, he would have had nothing, Partly, that was a matter of practicality; it was because she was a syphilitic whore that he could do her no harm, being infected with syphilis himself, whereas he would have been taking on a terrible burden of guilt had he deliberately taken up with any woman that was not, but that was only a superficial reason, as all pragmatic reasons are. The truth of his incapacity to escape loneliness lay deeper than that.

That realization—the realization about the metaphorical significance of the Devil's red cravat, I mean, and my induced theorizing about Baudelaire—was oddly discomfiting, and I realized that I was beginning to feel seriously queasy.

I watched the Devil drain his glass for what was probably the third or fourth time—he was more than half way down the bottle, which no longer had the label advertising it as Australian Shiraz, and from which, when he refilled his glass, the liquid pouring out was no longer red—and I suddenly felt an overpowering need to urinate, and fled from the room.

Nowadays, of course, when I'm an old age pensioner and afflicted by the kind of slow prostate cancer of which very few men of my age die, but by which far more than fifty per cent are afflicted, that feeling is commonplace, but in 1997 I had not yet turned fifty, and had yet to experience the majority of the symptoms of old age. For that reason, the need seemed like a symptom of a more serious malaise, and the conviction suddenly hit me, as I pissed urgently and copiously, that I really was ill, and that my poor body, laboring away beneath the reach of consciousness, was striving with all its might to get rid of something, to expel it from my being before it could do me any more harm.

I remembered something then that my sixth-form biology teacher, Francis Minns, had once told the class, while talking about processes of biological fermentation. The story is surely false, but, perhaps for that reason, it had stuck in my mind.

Siberian peasants, he said, sometimes did not bother with the tedious business of external fermentation as a means of producing drinkable alcohol. They simply swallowed as much raw grain as they could stomach, and as much yeast, lay down on top of the stove and went to sleep, turning their own gut into a bioreactor from which the alcohol could be absorbed as soon as it was produced. Serious addicts of intoxication, he suggested, would add agaric mushrooms to the mix, in order that the alcohol would be laced with hallucinogenic muscarine, for a real blast. And to cap it all, he told us, when they finally got up off the stove in order to urinate, they would drink their own piss, because their piss would be an alcohol/muscarine cocktail that would send them straight back into psychic orbit instead of allowing them to come back down to the direly frozen earth.

Unsurprisingly, I didn't feel the slightest temptation to drink my own piss, because I was beginning to feel a desperate, if perhaps a trifle belated, desire to come back down to earth. And I had already formed the conviction that, whether my piss had any alcohol in it or not—as I strongly suspected that it did, given that my metabolism was taking the hit from the Devil's drinking, even though my own lips hadn't touched a drop—the alcohol was not the more dangerous element of the cocktail.

What I had breathed in with the dust of Glofeydd Diafol, I was suddenly convinced, was not some organic refuse dating back to the Carboniferous Era. The soft coal dust had merely been the matrix on which a modern, contemporary fungus had grown while the books from the old pit library had been stewing in their boxes. What I had taken aboard was something *alive*, something multiplying and changing, which my immune system had taken three full days to overpower, and was only now beginning to devour and commit to my urine. In all probability, it would be out of my system completely in another couple of days or so, but in the meantime, my immune system was reacting in a perfectly conventional fashion, turning what had been a feeling of muted and mild malaise into a feverish crisis, sending my metabolism into overdrive.

It could have been worse. In fact, it could have been a lot worse. I'd seen the Devil, as individuals suffering from Saint Anthony's Fire were often reported to do, but I hadn't suffered any of the other awful symptoms of ergotism. Whatever the fungus was that I'd taken in, it wasn't nearly as nasty as *Claviceps purpurea*. I didn't have to fear convulsions, or gangrene. Even though I'd taken aboard a relatively massive dose, much greater than Martin's and very much greater than Penny's or Lionel's, my symptoms were relatively mild, even more benign than the slow cancers described by that term in medical jargon, like the ones growing at various points in my skin and the one that would soon begin to magnify my prostate and play havoc with my lower plumbing.

But still, it was a disease. It wasn't just a mild intoxication. The Devil was not my friend; no matter how much sympathy I might feel for him, in my perverse fashion, he was incapable of feeling any for me—and no matter how honest the pact he had made might be, the small print hidden in its darker regions cast severe doubts on its fairness.

On the other hand, fair or not, it was the only game in town, for the moment, and it was better than nothing. It was better than loneliness.

For that reason, when I went back to the front room, having readjusted my clothing and my attitude, and pulled myself together, I didn't want to find the Devil gone. I was hoping that he was still there, even though I now had some slight reason to be apprehensive about what might now be in that bottle from which he hadn't yet finished drinking, given that he had evidently worked some diabolical magic on it.

I sat down on the sofa again, and looked the Devil in the eye, meeting his unfathomable gaze, before looking at the bottle. I had bought it off the shelves in Asda, and had paid for it at the till without raising a flicker of surprise or interest. At that time, I was certain, it really had been a bottle of cheap Australian Shiraz, whose principal attraction had been the fact that it was on special offer.

Now, the bottle was black glass, of a kind that had never been seen on any supermarket shelf in England or anywhere else. The liquid in the Devil's glass was pale green.

I didn't have to ask him what it was; it was absinthe: not the sanitized produce bearing that name that you can nowadays buy easily, but the demonized version derived from the flowers and leaves of *Artemisia absinthium*—alias wormwood—flavored with green anise, fennel and a cocktail of supposedly medicinal herbs, which had been banned in France in 1915 as a danger to the war effort.

I sat down, and I smiled.

I smiled because I knew that absinthe's evil reputation was a myth, that it did not actually have the hallucinogenic properties that popular legend had credited to it, that wormwood was essentially harmless in moderate doses, and that the only harmful effects that absinthe had had in its heyday were entirely due to the high percentage of alcohol therein, which were effectively nullified if it was drunk, as most people actually had drunk it, mixed with liberal quantities of water. In Paris, in fact, where its evil reputation had been forged, the water had probably been more dangerous than the absinthe itself, and putting too much water in the mix, thus preserving a fraction of its native infestations from the bactericidal effects of the alcohol, had probably caused the worst of its reputed side-effects.

"I really am going to have a hangover in the morning," I told him. "You lied about that. I don't know what else you lied about, but you definitely don't tell the truth all the time."

The Devil shook his head, in feeble negation. "I can't foresee the future," he said, probably telling the truth. "I had no way of knowing whether you would have a hangover or not. Telling you that you wouldn't was making a statement that was certainly unwarranted, but there was at least a possibility that the power of suggestion would help it to come true. I can't claim to have done it with the best of intentions, as doctors do when they lie through their teeth by telling people that they're going to get better in the hope of mobilizing the placebo effect, but the business of telling the truth isn't quite the black-and-white issue that it's made out to be. If it will help you feel better, though—although I can't imagine why it would—I can assure you that you'll definitely have a hangover tomorrow morning."

"For the moment," I confessed, "I'm more worried about the possibility that if you finish drinking that bottle of absinthe, given that it must contain at least as much alcohol as three bottles of wine, I'm probably going to start vomiting again."

The Devil smiled wryly. "Probably," he agreed—but he didn't stop sipping from his glass.

"So, I said," if you have any more questions to ask, perhaps you ought to ask them now, before we're interrupted again." Somehow, I knew that he wasn't going to stick around once I started throwing up, even if I managed to get to the sink this time. Nor did I have any confidence that I'd ever see him again, now that my immune system was winning the war against the invader.

"The pact is formally satisfied," he told me.

I didn't question the insertion of the adverb. I knew that he couldn't be satisfied other than formally, but that he was a sufficiently honest dealer to settle for enlightenment he'd obtained from me, meager as it might be. That cut both ways, but I was an honest dealer too; not only wasn't I about to demand any more than I'd been granted, I was prepared to figure that I'd got the better half of the exchange. I knew that I'd learned a lot more from our little chats than he had—inevitably given that I had so much more capacity for change and evolution than he had. He knew far too much already, and had the entire burden of the past weighing him down with a kind of inertia I could scarcely imagine.

"I know you can't predict the future," I said, "and I know that I'd be a perfect fool to ask about mine, because I've read far too many stories of oracular perversity to imagine than anyone could possible derive any real benefit from precognition, but, speaking merely as a serious student of probability, do you think I have even the slightest chance remaining of making a belated success of my life?"

"No," he said, with perfect honesty.

"Do you have any advice as to what I might do about that?"

"Yes," he said. "Do nothing. There's nothing you can do."

"You wouldn't recommend suicide, then?"

"Of course not. The only time it's worth committing suicide is when you shouldn't."

"What do you mean?"

"It's a corollary of the Silenus paradox: the best thing of all is not to be born, and after that to die young, but by the time anyone is capable of realizing that, it's too late. The only way that suicide can save you from a life of humiliation, pain and failure is before you start living, but before you start living, you have no way of knowing that that's the kind of future that awaits you, because it's inherently unpredictable. The only time that you can be sure that committing suicide will spare you anything is when you have nothing left to spare, by which time there's no point. As I say, there's nothing you can do. The odds are stacked against you, but you still have to play your hand with the cards you're dealt. No matter how crappy your hand is, it's better than nothing. And even if you feel as if you're walking through life with your head cut off, all you can do is put on a ghoulish cravat and keep walking. That's life."

"Not for you," I pointed out, even though he was the one with the red cravat.

"Do you envy me my condition?" he asked, evidently not quite having run out of questions, even though the formal requirements of our pact had apparently been satisfied.

It was a good question. Did I envy him the existential condition of being unable to feel grief and sorrow, love and hate, misery and joy? Did I envy him eternity, devoid of sleep and dreams? Did I envy him being trapped in the existential necessary of being the antithesis of the Creator, even if the Creator wasn't by any means what he was cracked up to be by his avid fans, and was, in fact, a sorry mess of vanity and vexation of spirit?"

"I'm not sure that I can answer that right now," I said.

"I know," he said. "That's why I didn't ask before. I can't predict the future, but I suspect that you never will be able to make up your mind on that one."

There was no point asking him whether he envied me. He didn't. He couldn't. The root source of all seven of the deadly sins, he couldn't feel any of them. If he had been capable of envy, could he possibly have envied any human condition, even one as paltry as mine? It was a meaningless question, to which no answer was possible.

"For the time being," I told him, "I'm not going to tell anyone that I've seen you or talked to you, mainly because they'd think I was insane, and could be right, but also because I'd like to mull over the ideas that you've stimulated for a while, especially as they might yet be supplemented by the produce of Axel Castle's experiment. When the time eventually comes, however, given that it undoubtedly will, given what I am, do you have any objection to my writing down an honest account of this interview? Obviously, I'll have to represent it as frivolous fiction, tending to the surrealist and the absurd, but even so...."

"Feel free," he said. "Publish and be damned." He just couldn't resist, and I couldn't blame him.

"Thanks," I said. "I'll try my damnedest to remember everything accurately, in spite of the side-effects of the fungus."

His only reply to that was to raise his glass in mock salute. The absinthe was almost gone.

"You know," I told him, "not only are you not really here and not really drinking that, but it's not really absinthe, and absinthe doesn't really have the effects that are credited to it by its demonic reputation. All that's *really* happening here is that I'm drinking a bottle of cheap Australian Shiraz, on my own, because I'm a blocked writer temporarily reduced to utter helplessness. The rest is just layers of illusion, provoked by the microscopic spores of some uncatalogued fungus nourished on the velvety black dust of Glofeydd Diafol."

"I know," he said, "but what would life be worth without fantasy? And what would fantasy be worth without vivid imagination, without the comical, the quirky, the absurd and the surreal? Sane, no doubt, but really, *really* dull, as only reality can be."

And with that, the sense of gathering nausea reached the threshold at which I had to make a bolt for the downstairs loo. I made it in time, but the rest of that night, so far as I can remember anything about it, was one of those intervals over which a writer has the fortunate prerogative of what is known in the parlance of the métier as "drawing a veil."

CHAPTER XII

I hardly got out of bed for the next few days, mostly just to go and piss more fungal toxin away, get myself jugs of water so that I wouldn't get dehydrated, and make myself a cup of cocoa when it got dark. I think I had a bad time, but my memory has obligingly blotted most of it out, so that I can't remember any details at all—except for the bizarre run-up, when I saw the Devil, of which I retained, and still retain, *every* detail. I suspect that that would have been one of the clauses in the fine print of the pact, if it had had any small print—or, indeed, any print at all.

By Saturday, however, I was up and about again, if a trifle zombified, and by Sunday I was feeling normal again—which is to say that I was my usual depressed, obsessive and compulsively flippant self: normal for me, if not for the proverbial man in the street.

On Monday, I actually went back to work, or tried. I forced myself to sit at the machine for several hours before I gave up and devoted myself to reading. Although I didn't actually write anything substantial, I did rack my brains and peck out half a dozen story ideas that might possibly be worth developing—not the next day, obviously, as I was committed to be in Pontypridd, but once I was able to get back to serious, sustained and authentically productive labor, hewing away at the word-face like a conscientious intellect-miner.

I deliberately tried to keep the ideas I was throwing up as light as possible, free-associating ideas and not applying any kind of rational mental triage. I knew from experience that it was a method that mostly produced rubbish, but that the rubbish was usually compensated by the emergence of one or two viable ideas extractable from the matrix and capable of rational extrapolation and polishing. Although my production of potentially-saleable wordage remained at zero, I did get some serious reading done, and I wasn't dissatisfied with my day's labor.

I had lower standards in those days. Now that I'm finally beginning to get a grip on my craft, I wouldn't tolerate such idleness and lack of focus, but these things take practice, and thirty years isn't necessarily a long apprenticeship in this line of work.

In the evening I ate a hearty and relatively healthy meal, which probably did me a lot of good and certainly went some way to repairing the deficit I'd accumulated during my days of inertia and convalescence. Afterwards, I packed my traveling-bag for my trip to Wales.

I hesitated over which CDs I ought to take with me, wondering whether I ought to broaden out the range, or even stick entirely to the brighter end of the spectrum, but in the end I decided that I might as well go the whole Gothic hog, so I packed Fields of the Nephilim's *Elizium* and *Revelations*, the Garden of Delight's *Necromanteion IV* and Sopor Aeternus and the Ensemble of Shadows' *Dead Lovers' Sarabande*. I figured that if they couldn't get me in the mood for a defiant confrontation with the Cosmic Mind, nothing would. As a concession to more Romantic exoticism, I also packed Ataraxia's *Lost Atlantis*, just in case, but I resisted the temptation to add Meat Loaf's *Bat out of Hell* to the collection, because it was too theatrical.

The train journey the next morning wasn't too bad, except for the connection that went from Cardiff to Pontypridd. I spent the time productively, reading Villiers de l'Isle Adam's *Tribulat Bonhomet*. It isn't easy to read French texts without a dictionary to hand, but making up English equivalents for all the French words you don't know is always a stimulating exercise, and you can revel in the faint but exciting possibility that the text you've partly-improvised might actually be an improvement on the original. Then again, it was a lot better for the image than reading *Viz*.

Lionel was waiting to meet me, as promised, with two companions, who were apparently interested to meet me even though there was no need for them to have made the effort. Actually, they'd turned up fifteen minutes late, but so had the train. I find that life is replete with such wonderful coincidences, even when I'm not slightly late for an appointment with the Cosmic Mind; I expect that everyone else does too.

"This is Claire," said Lionel, introducing the taller of his two companions. "And this is Axel, who spoke to you on the phone." I had a brief impression of *déjà-vu* as I compared Axel and Claire mentally with Martin and Penny, although the similarity stopped at number and sex. I must have been getting old even then, because Alex and Claire seemed seriously young to me, in spite of the fact that they had to have their doctorates already in the bag and were pretending as hard as they could to look like serious scientists. Axel even had a tweed jacket that wouldn't quite button up over his overly plump belly, and Claire had glasses with blue-tinted lenses the size of coasters.

"Hi," I said to them both. "How's the getting-in-touch business going? I'm glad to see that Lionel at least, hasn't been turned into a gibbering wreck yet by the sheer Lovecraftian cosmic horror of realizing man's absolute insignificance within the unutterable bleakness of the universe."

Lionel beamed, as a man with God on his side, who has no fear of the revelations of the dark mind, is surely entitled to do. Axel managed a faint grin, but Claire frowned, obviously disapproving of the irreverence.

"Let me rephrase that," I said, not really trying very hard to sound contrite. "How did the first experimental run go?"

"We can't discuss any other experimental runs," Claire said, sternly, as the four of us clambered into a dark blue Hyundai. "There are important issues of confidentiality as well as a danger of prejudicing your expectations—and in any case, we've hardly started." She had got into the driver's seat, so I assumed that it was her car. Lionel got into the front passenger seat, so I was left to share the back with Axel.

"It's not for me to tell you what attitude to take to the experiment, Dr. Stableford," Axel said, hypocritically, "but do try to bear in mind that this isn't a joke to us. The research is genuinely new, because nobody has ever had the necessary computing power before, let alone the kind of programs we're using to collate and analyze the data. For obvious reasons, we can't know what we're going to find, but we really do think that we have a real chance of delving further into the unconscious part of the mind than any kind of hypnotism or transcendental meditation has so far been able to do."

"Oh, I agree," I assured him. "If there is a key that will enable to you open that door, the power of music is the most logical place to look for it. I should probably have stopped there, but I was feeling a little light-minded, so I let myself ramble on. "If your computer program really does allow you not merely to map the brain's responses to favorite music but redesign it so as to enhance the effect," I mused, "you might actually get to the *terra incognita* of the dark mind. Reverse all the way from the cerebrum into the hind-brain, turn left at the hypothalamus and drive a mine-shift straight down the spinal cord to oblivion, as it were. On the other hand, unraveling four billion years of mental evolution, chucking the mental strata of civilization, animality, and vegetation on the nearest slag-heap, following the dark seam until it peters out into the gaseous flow and fizz of the ultraconsciousness of cyanobacterial slime...well, I suspect that might take a little longer. It might be unwise to expect too much too soon. Trance and dance might only equal spiritual strip-tease...achieving orgasmic contact might be a long way off yet."

"Very colorfully put, Dr. Stableford," said Axel, sounding like a man who preferred his colors in pastel shades.

"When you spoke to me on the phone," I reminded him, "you did suggest that you might be willing to tell me a little more about the theory that's guiding your research. I'd be interested to hear it, if you think it won't prejudice my anticipations too much."

Alex glanced at the back of his collaborator's head, but she was busy watching the busy road, along which the traffic flow was distinctly awkward; she wouldn't have been able to shoot him a censorious glance even if she wanted to. "No," he said, "I don't think talking about the kind of theory we've sketched out will introduce any bias into the experiment, as long as we don't get too specific. Are you, by any chance familiar with the thesis that the brain, rather than generating consciousness, actually restricts it?"

"Sure," I said. It takes more than a twenty-something psychologist from the University of Glamorgan to put me on the wrong intellectual foot, especially when my mind is in a nimble mood. "The fact that you're bandying about the term 'Cosmic Mind' is rather suggestive in itself. One version of the rhetoric built around that catch-phrase derives from Lamarckian and Bergsonian evolutionary theory, suggesting that the fundamental sentience of the universe permeates everything, providing a kind of elementary teleological impulse. Although primitive organisms, in that view, aren't individually conscious, they nevertheless participate in some infinitesimally small way in the vast motion of a universal train of mentality, of which thought and feeling are among the more advanced manifestations.

"As primitive brains become more advanced, though, they evolve so as gradually to isolate the individual from the cosmic mind-stream, enclosing and usurping a little of its potential, which can be organized and formulated as a *self*...eventually, when brains become as skillful as human brains, into a self-conscious self, which naturally comes to the conclusion that it's independent and self-contained—perhaps even alone, if it's solipsistically inclined—even though it's really only the feeblest echo of that from which it has been incompletely extracted. Although ignorant of its true nature and origin, it nevertheless retains an intuition of the Whole and can't help yearning for reconnection, even though the price of that reconnection would be the effective annihilation of the individual.

"If it only had the evolutionist input to sustain it, the theory would have petered out like the Welsh mining industry, but the notion has been somewhat rebooted by physicists hung up on the uncertainty principle. If observers are required in order to collapse wave-functions and bring concrete events out of the hesitant fuzz of subatomic potentiality, the reasoning goes, the universe must have required an observing consciousness long before we—or even cyanobacteria—first evolved. In that way of thinking, some form of Universal Consciousness is an elementary condition of existence. Thus, quantum mechanics can take on the role of deism to *élan vital*'s theism. Is that about it?"

"That's an interesting way of putting it," said Axel, apparently sincerely.

"No it isn't," said Claire Louchon, cool as a cucumber behind her blue shades, with her eyes still religiously fixed on the route ahead—which was necessary as we were now in a rather convoluted part of the town center, where progress was exceedingly difficult. "It's contemptuous, oversimplified crap, which doesn't begin to do justice to the notion of the implicate order, the quantum-computer theory of intelligence or the essential paradoxicality of voluntarism. You don't need to humor this one, Axel. He's not some drug-addled lap-dancer—he's a professional smartarse."

I was mildly insulted by that. Back in 1997 I could adjust my jargon to circumstance as well as any other intellectual chameleon, and I could drop names such as David Bohm and Roger Penrose with the best of them, if I felt the need. If the occasion were sufficiently desperate, I could even masquerade as a postmodernist for at least twenty minutes without cracking a smile. I was, however, interested by the implication that one of their previous experimental subjects might been a drug-addled lap-dancer. I might have followed that up if Claire hadn't already pulled up, while she was still tearing me off a strip, at the hotel where I'd apparently be staying.

"We'll get you checked in and give you ten minutes to freshen up," Lionel said. "Then we'll meet you in the lobby and take you out to the lab. Bring the CDs down with you."

Claire and Axel stayed in the car while Lionel accompanied me to the hotel desk. "It's going to be bad enough having to sit in a chair for hours on end with cloven ping pong balls over my eyes," I told him, once we were safely out of earshot, "without having to be insulted as well. Or are they just running a good cop/bad cop routine to soften me up? I didn't think experimental psychologists went in for intensive interrogation techniques."

"You started it," he reminded me.

I took his point, and nodded, in a quasi-apologetic fashion. I conceded that my cavalier urge to show off had led me to be a trifle unkind to poor Axel, and that Claire had probably only been trying to restore the balance, in a spirit of fair play. I resolved to be more courteous in future, although I knew that it wasn't a resolution I'd find it easy to keep.

"I saw Martin yesterday, by the way," said Lionel. "He says that he felt seriously sick for a couple of days, but he's better now. He hasn't had any further trouble with paranormal phenomena and discomfiting presences, but he's decided to get rid of the shop anyway, once he's tidied it up so that he can try to sell it on as a going concern. He reckons that he's not cut out to be a book dealer. He told me that he hadn't quite realized what a world of difference there is between being a reader and being a real bookman, and that he's obviously just a reader. He thinks he might look for a little newsagent's shop, or a pizza franchise."

"Good luck to him," I said. "Have you heard from Penny?"

"I've talked to her on the phone. She felt rough too, for a while, but she must be okay now. She was away up the valleys over the weekend, probably on some enquiry for the SPR. More promising ground for hauntings there than in Barry, from what I've seen. The rural Welsh are more firmly rooted in their native soil, more closely in touch with their ancestors, and far too wise to doubt the nearness of the Other World."

"Good luck to her, too," I said. "She phoned to tell me that she was feeling off color earlier in the week, but I guess she must have made a full recovery. At any rate, she didn't phone again. How about you?"

He beamed. "Still skating on that thin crust called reality," he assured me, quoting the catch-phrase he used back then in every episode of *Fortean TV*. "You won't believe some of the stuff we're lining up for the next series," he added. "Be sure to watch it, won't you?"

"Actually, Lionel," I told him, "I won't believe any of it. But I'll tune in religiously just the same."

"It'll be worth it," he assured me.

I assumed that he was conscientiously avoiding the subject of what he had experienced during the run of Alex and Claire's experiment, because he had promised them not to tell me anything that might influence my expectations.

"Where did you find your two pet psychologists?" I enquired, after I'd finished filling in the registration card at the desk. "And why on earth do they think that it'll help their careers to form an association with the presenter of *Fortean TV*?"

"They found me," he explained, as the hotel clerk rooted around for an appropriate key, "but I doubt that they've ever seen *Fortean TV*. They heard me on local radio and thought I might be able to put them in touch with useful subjects. They move in much narrower social circles than I do—they're university people through and through."

The staff of jumped-up ragtag institutions like the so-called University of Glamorgan tended to take their newly-conferred status very seriously in those days, and often had serious ambitions to be "university people through and through." I knew the type.

"Useful subjects like me and the addled lap-dancer?" I queried.

"They did ask me to cast around for a broad spectrum," he confirmed, serenely. "You're a kind of balancing factor. The one that Claire refers to as a lap-dancer wasn't one of mine, though—I think she was a university graduate that Alex knew from his own undergrad days. She was just helping them out with the preliminary testing, but you'll be part of the actual experimental run."

The clerk finally handed me an electronic key card and I looked for the stairs—I was only on the first floor, so it wasn't worth taking the elevator.

"See you back at the car in ten minutes," Lionel said, as I started upstairs, and he turned away.

"Not a moment longer," I promised.

In fact, I was two minutes late, not because I need any more freshening up than the next man but because I'd taken a few minutes out while contemplating the walls of my dismal hotel room to wonder why I had come all the way to Pontypridd for a lousy fifty quid and a lecture from a snotty chit in comic glasses.

Real people, I had thought, *don't work for fees as miserable as that. On the other hand*, I had added, *in pursuit of my own principle of fair play, anyone who's been a professional writer for thirty-odd years has financial standards some way below floor-level, and writers are also the only people in the world who can spend time productively while sitting in a comfy chair with cloven ping pong balls taped over their eyes and whatever hair they have left tidily gathered into an electrode-rich hairnet.*

Maybe, I thought, my fictitious genetic engineers could follow up their first philosophical triumphs by producing further hosts of bookworms of the kind envisaged in the aborted story I'd abandoned before the diabolical fungus got into its stride, designed to convert psychology textbooks into more traditional collections of fairy tales, self-help manuals into dictionaries and the *Fortean Times* into *Viz*.

The landscape we drove through as we made our way out of town still bore the scars of a thousand years of mining, but none of the pits was active any more and the slag-heaps were slowly being reclaimed by heroic weeds. Whatever coal was still beneath us was distributed in all manner of inconvenient seams, whose exploitation was no longer economic. The pits could have gone deeper, but it wasn't worth the trouble—not, at least, until supplies of natural gas ran out, and probably never. For the time being, the people of the valleys had to scrape a living on the surface, where everything was dingy green and slate grey instead of honest pitch-black.

We drove past three more abandoned pitheads and five unconvincingly-reclaimed slagheaps on the way to the isolated university site that housed the lab where Claire and Axel committed their meager research grants to the Great Academic Drain. For some reason, the sight reminded me of my youth, when I used to sit atop Bingley Moor with my cousin Keith and look out over the Aire Valley at all the busy mills and chimneys belching black smoke into the sky. Last time I'd been back to the neighborhood, Salt's Mill had enjoyed sole dominion for miles around, preserved against the march of progress by its conversion into a David Hockney Museum.

The lab into which I was eventually ushered had a bad case of the Frankenstein syndrome. As Oscar Wilde obligingly pointed out, life imitates art far more frequently and far more assiduously than art imitates life, so, ever since James Whale dressed the set of Colin Clive's monster-factory, real-world laboratories have been trying hard to emulate it. The chair didn't look too intimidating, in spite of the network of electrodes draped over the head-rest and the electroencephalograph stationed behind it, and the sound-system wouldn't have looked out of place in a yuppie's loft, but the other apparatus—the one presumably responsible for the non-invasive "further phase" that Axel had left carefully unspecified—looked seriously weird. It put me in mind of a 1920s radio set designed by Salvador Dali in the course of a particularly bad acid trip.

"What's that?" I asked, pointing to a particularly enigmatic electronic gizmo.

"It's the olfactory equivalent of the synthesizer and mixer," Claire said, with brutal oversimplicity.

I guessed right away that she meant the synthesizer and mixer in the sound system, which would be used to fuse my music with the "hypnostream tape," but it took me a moment or two to figure out what the "olfactory equivalent" of that must be, and to realize that music wasn't the only key that they intended to use in their attempt to unlock the secret doors of perception. No drugs, they had said…but perhaps they were justified in not thinking of olfactory delivery as a matter of chemical enhancement.

"You mean that it synthesizes and mixes odors," I said. "A refinement of the sort of thing supermarkets use to pipe fresh bread smells onto the sales floor."

"That's right," said Axel. "Food science has come on by leaps and bounds in the last ten years, and much of what we think of as taste is really smell. I'm not allowed to tell you which of the big food company's R & D people loaned it to us, but it's what they call an *experiential enhancer*. The idea is…."

"I get the idea," I assured him. "Smell is the most primitive of the senses—the one that can dive down into your psyche to the deep strata of memory. It's like Proust and the Madeleine, except that you want to go deeper than that, beyond the lost time of childhood into layers of fossilized race-memory, where the rich black anthracite of eternity is stored…allegedly."

"Well," said Axel, dropping the good cop act for the first time, and sounding slightly annoyed by my turn of phrase, "that's not quite…."

"Leave it, Axel," Claire said. "Let's not plant any suggestions."

"God forbid," I said. "Oh—sorry, Lionel." I figured that as an ordained minister in the Church of Wales, Lionel evidently had his own ideas about the nature and opinions of the Cosmic Mind, whether or not he'd been able to have a chat with it—Him, in his view—while he was doing his own stint in the comfy chair. I couldn't help wondering whether he'd caught the scent of God—or, indeed, a slight whiff of brimstone—but I couldn't ask, in case Claire Louchon started accusing him of planting suggestions.

"No problem," Lionel said, in response to my mock-apology, manifesting his invariable generosity and tolerance.

"Well," said Claire, as she studied the five CDs I'd handed over to her, "I can see that you're not intimidated by the possibility of being turned into a gibbering wreck by Lovecraftian cosmic horror."

"If I wanted to go that way," I said, not sparing the sarcasm, on the grounds that she evidently wasn't, "I'd have brought *Andy Williams' Greatest Hits, Perry Como Sings the Blues*, and *Songs from the Best Broadway Musicals of 1959*. I don't actually have anything by Kylie or Robbie Williams." I didn't actually have the three titles I'd named, either, but that didn't seem particularly relevant to the point I was making.

Before they invited me to sit in the comfy chair and applied the shards of the ruined ping pong ball Axel showed me the last item of relevant equipment: a miniature dictaphone whose mike would be clipped to the collar of my shirt. "Say anything you like," he said. "We're not expecting a running commentary on your experiences, although you can do that if you like, and we probably won't include any verbal reportage in our write-up, which will focus on the objective record of your brain activity. It's just a matter of covering the angles."

Personally, I would have thought that any "verbal reportage" their subjects could give them would be far more interesting than the mere "objective" record of alpha- beta-, delta- and theta-waves as recorded by the electroencephalograph, but I'm a writer.

All I said, however, was: "Shouldn't you include all your results in your write-up?" It was a silly question, though; scientific journals hate messy data; they like numerical data, because numerical data looks far more "scientific." If Axel and Claire wanted their research grant extended or renewed, the graphic jiggles on the electroencephalograph would be their principal selling point.

"If we manage to send your brain into the state we hope to achieve," Axel informed me, with a slight sigh, "the subjective experience will probably be indescribable—at least to begin with. It doesn't matter—the machine will keep track of your mental states and will tell us when you reach what hypnotists used to call the somnambulistic state, although I don't like the term. We don't expect you to get out of the state of normal consciousness for today, while we're just measuring reactions, but the crucial test of my program is what we get tomorrow, when we feed you the adapted tape. Then, we shouldn't have any difficulty reaching the somniloquent state, and which point it will be help full if you can say something, no matter what, just to confirm the state. It might well seem like nonsense, but …."

"Too much information," Claire snapped, censoriously.

Axel blushed, but made an attempt to assert his independence by carrying on regardless. "In the longer term, of course...," he began, but the glare of the tinted lenses withered caused him hesitate momentarily.

"What longer term?" I asked, surprised. "I thought tomorrow was the end."

"It is, for now," Alex continued, obviously having steeled himself, "but once we've demonstrated that the system can enable all the subjects to reach the desired level of relaxation—the somniloquent state, that being a better term than somnambulistic, as there isn't any ambulation involved— and we've got the grant extension, we'll invite them back again for the next phase. This is intended to be phase one of a long-term project, although we'll obviously have to get the requisite grant support if we're to continue it as we'd like. Any further participation will obviously be up to you, of course, but we hope that at least some of the participants in this first experimental run will find it interesting...."

"On the other hand," Claire Louchon put in, presumably interrupting because she couldn't see any other way of getting him to shut up, "we won't necessarily invite them, back, even if they are interested. We're not making any promises, any more than we're asking you for any."

I gathered that she was not optimistic about my proving to be useful subject, given that she had already written me off as a wisecracking smartarse. She probably had much higher hopes of Penny from the SPR— although I couldn't help wondering, now, whether things had gone as smoothly with Lionel as they'd hoped, or were still prepared to pretend.

"How long will you go on, if you can get the funding?" I asked Alex.

"As long as the funding lasts," he replied, logically enough. "We're really excited about this. If everything goes well, and you were interested in continuing, and we can get the funding, we'd probably want to sign you up for monthly sessions over a year and a half. We'll bring in more sophisticated apparatus as and when we can, and work out a more elaborate system of reportage. The pay's lousy, as you know—but it'll be interesting work, if everything goes well."

There seemed to be a lot of big ifs in there, but he was young and entitled to maintain his brainchild with all the enthusiasm he could muster.

"But what if your system doesn't manage to put me into this 'somniloquent' state," I asked—worried for him, not for me.

"Well, we'll have to see about that," Alex said. "Personally, I'm glad to have the opportunity to try it out on a skeptic, who has proved resistant to pre-existent methods. That's the real test, after all. If we only recruited people who are not only suggestible but who go in expecting to gain profitable insights of some kind...."

"Fair enough," I said. "I'll keep my skepticism ready to hand, but I won't bring it to bear in advance—I'll do my best to cooperate, but I can't make any promises. Mind like a nuclear bunker."

Alex smiled. He obviously had faith in his machines go get a grip on my brain waves, whatever I thought about the likelihood of that. "Don't worry," he said. "The EEG will tell us what's really going on, no matter what extremes of denial your self-consciousness resorts to. Is it okay if I put the blinders on, now?"

I glanced sideways at Lionel, who grinned broadly and gave me a thumbs-up sign. Claire was fiddling with the EEG equipment, but the way the light was reflecting off her blue-tinted glasses would have made it difficult to know whether she was meeting my eye even if she had been that way inclined.

"Fire away," I said, relaxing into the comfy chair and closing my eyes.

"From now on," Axel said, "just forget we're here."

"No problem," I assured him, manifesting my own not-quite-invariable generosity and tolerance.

CHAPTER XIII

The first phase of the relaxation tape consisted of a heartbeat set against a background of quasi-oceanic white noise. I'd heard similar things before, and the thinking behind it was easy enough to understand; it was supposed to recapitulate the preconscious but unforgotten experience of an embryo in the womb, which we are all supposed to carry within us, in the remotest depths of our memories, no matter how old we become or how comprehensively divorced from the primitive roots of our own inner being. At nearly fifty, I was a little further removed from my ancestral child than your average drug-addled lap dancer, but that only meant that I would need a little more exposure. In time, I knew that Axel would start feeding in familiar melodies to complement and complicate the fundamental rhythm without overwhelming it.

It occurred to me that blending the essential sounds of Mummy Dearest and the Tinnitus of Time with the Fields of the Nephilim and the Gardens of Delight—not to mention Ataraxia and Sopor Aeternus, aided and inspired by the Ensemble of Shadows—might produce some strange results. Running through the names like that made me realize that my selections hadn't been at all inappropriate to the task in hand—probably better, I flattered myself by thinking, than anything that Lionel or the terrible two's other hapless subjects would be able to come up with.

I wasn't afraid of becoming bored, even if the relaxation tape had no measurable effect at all. One of the few advantages of accepting a vocation as a writer, apart from licensing various kinds of obsessive/compulsive behavior, is that boredom becomes impossible. When you have nothing else to occupy your mind, you can get down to serious work—in fact, you can't help but get down to serious work.

You don't actually have to make a mental resolution to start plotting; it happens anyway. A little bit of conscious guidance and a certain amount of extrapolative discipline help to nudge the process in more productive directions, but they aren't strictly necessary. Nor do you need to carry your "ideas file" around in your head ready for flicking through; a fertile mind might grow nothing but weeds if it's too long unattended, but they spring up in much greater profusion than they do on the average mental compost-heap. There's always something pushing up through a writer's mental subsoil, hungry for the rays of the interior sun, and if you root through it long enough, you'll always come up with something usable. The fact that I'd spent much of the previous day free-associating in order to generate potential ideas for development, the wackier the better, gave me a mental stock ready to hand.

I tried to select out a few that might actually make the substance of new stories to add to my long series of "tales of the biotech revolution," which I'd been turning out for more than a decade. I'd used up all the obvious ideas and plot-twists, and was finding it increasingly difficult to find new wrinkles.

With the previous day's mental capital fresh in hand, I started thinking about the possibility that mice genetically engineered as disease-models might be persuaded in future to be increasingly better mimics of human disorders, perhaps to the point of being "homunculized" by clever embryological manipulation.

Then I began to wonder what might happen as the pressure of need required the homunculi to get larger and more sophisticated in order to provide more accurate simulations of the human brain, and to what new hazards they might be subjected, especially in the context in their use for testing defenses against possible plague war warfare. How intelligent might they become, I wondered, and at what point would the ethical problems involved in custom-designing guinea-pigs designed to die of nasty diseases become particularly acute?

One of the standard principles of designing a plot to fit around and contain a sciencefictional idea is to ask the question: "Who will get hurt?" so I tried to figure out more elaborate casts of characters, in order that more hurt would be at stake than that of the homunculi themselves, given that it probably wouldn't be reasonable or desirable to use one of them as a viewpoint character. I wondered whether I could spin the details of the plot in such a way as to license borrowing "I am the very model of a modern Major-General" from *The Pirates of Penzance* as a title....

While I was thinking about that, I gradually paid less attention to the music track, although the experimenters had already begun to mix tracks from my own CDs into the relaxation tape. I was certain that I hadn't even begun to relax yet, in the technical sense of the term, but I tried to put that out of my mind in order to give the experiment a fair chance of making progress. The familiarity of the tracks made them easy enough to relegate them to the backcloth of thought, which I assume that Axel and Claire wanted me to do, so they could monitor the brain's reaction to them with the mediation of conscious attention reduced to a minimum.

After letting the first story idea run on at an easy pace for a while, I switched tack and started thinking about the possibility of writing a story about the future of biopiracy, which I had long wanted to do. The idea had attracted a certain amount of topical attention recently, because multinational pharmaceutical companies had begun methodically searching through the folk-medicines of the Third World, looking for therapeutically-useful compounds which they could then refine and patent, thus claiming all the profits for themselves. A certain amount of indignation was probably in order, and it did add certain something to the tragedy of the American genocides to imagine how rich the surviving natives of that continent might be if they were permitted nowadays to collect a royalty on sales of quinine, let alone tobacco and the potato.

I wondered if I could represent the future of the situation dramatically, in metaphorical terms, by imagining the multinationals sending out "privateers" running riot throughout the third world in search of Eldorados of biotech treasure, harassed in the meantime by local buccaneers, who hawked their preserved goods in some kind of futuristic Tortuga, as well as law enforcement agents eager to regulate the trade. I speculated as whether it might be worth using *The Second Coming of Columbus* as a title in order to focus on hypothetical Caribbean biopiracy, and whether, if I did, it might be worth introducing a whole new breed of ecoterrorists determined not to repeat the errors of the ill-fated Carib Indians.

Who, in that case, I asked my Muse, might be able to play Friday to some kind of metaphorical Crusoe, stranded on an island where some kind of biotech motherlode happened to have evolved, in accordance with the typical idiosyncrasy of the differentiation of island populations? On the other hand, I thought, it might to be better to exploit the Byronic imagery of *The Corsair*, or even the Wagneresque brio of *The Flying Dutchman*, if I wanted to stay upmarket, provided that I could think of a crime sufficiently unusual to justify some such punishment....

Commercially, of course, the sensible thing would be to think of cinematic pirates rather than operatic ones, but that might be too restrictive, and also less Romantic...but the crucial thing about the story wasn't that kind of decorative material anyway; what it really needed, as a narrative anchorage, was a first-rate object of piracy, a biotechnological prize that would generate an adequate competition, without being a mere arbitrary McGuffin....

It wasn't until that point in my musing, strangely enough, that I first noticed the contribution of Axel's odor-machine. Whether it was because he'd held it back until my EEG trace suggested that I was in a receptive mood or because my everpresent allergic rhinitis had preventing me from smelling the introductory suite of odors, I had no idea. The first odor I recognized, however, was wood smoke, followed by frying bacon, baking smells and floral scents.

To begin with, the scent-track was distracting, but I tried to relegate it to be background along with the music. I suspect that I failed, because I couldn't help trying to look for the logic of the streaming. It would be claiming too much to say that I recognized all the odors, but a sequence soon began which had a suggestion of dry and slightly acrid grass, with a slight seasoning of musk and shit. It didn't take a genius to work out that Axel might trying to recapitulate the perfume of the African savannah, where our remote ancestors had first evolved as primal biotechnologists, developing all the tools and skills required for cooking and making clothes.

Then the odors faded again, or became too difficult to classify. Either way, I eventually lost interest and went back to work.

I began thinking about the possibility of writing a story about human chimeras, compounded as early embryos out of egg-cells donated by as many as eight or twelve genetically-enhanced parents, which might allow the aggregate households of the emortality-challenged future to conserve a biological relationship between the parents and the children. Then I wondered what might happen if the various cell-stocks began a kind of battle to constitute the different tissues and organs of the chimerical individual, and how the eight or twelve parents might feel as they monitored the results of that conflict and witnessed the progress and settlements of a kind of natural selection that had never had a chance to occur before.

I began to examine the possibilities deducible from the hypothesis that the conflict might be able reach resolutions previously unimagined, if the chimerical wholes began manufacturing transposons in order to facilitate their own internal gene-trading mechanisms. That kind of natural selection might give a sudden boost to the pace of human evolution, and deflect it into new directions, especially if gene-sculptors remained actively involved, suppressing some developments and enhancing others, perhaps competitively....

The odors seemed to have faded away completely by the time that idea had run its course, presumably because Axel had run through the entire sequence whose neurological responses he wanted to track. The music was still playing, but for the first time, the songs that had previously been played in their entirety began to be broken down, presumably in order to get a more detailed account of the nature and pattern of my brain's reflexive responses. The fragmentation, like the introduction of the odors, was disturbing to begin with, but again, it didn't take long for me to get used to it and to pay less attention.

Then I wasted a little time on trivia, wondering whether cultures currently practicing surgical clitoridectomy might become interested in taking advantage of a rapid increase of expertise in embryonic engineering to request that their female children should be modified in the womb in such a way that that they wouldn't require any such surgical operation. What effects, I asked myself, hypothetically, might that have on the consequent generation of declitorized female infants when they grew to adulthood?

If ambitious chimerization became possible at the same time as sophisticated embryonic engineering, I thought, other forms of embryonic engineering might become possible. Was it possible, I wondered, that lycanthropy might one day become fashionable? And if it ever did, what would then happen if the artificial werewolves' innate gene-trading systems began to exercise a distinct preference for wolfishness…in much the same way that the embryonically-modified clitoris-free children might decide to take charge of their own future development and evolution by continuing the process which their blinkered parents had only begun, without even bothering to wonder what further consequences there might be once the snowball started rolling.…

I got a whiff of something slightly noxious at that point, which put me in mind of a Lovecraftian shoggoth, but somewhere in the distance, Francesca Nicoli of Ataraxia was singing the dolphin song from *Lost Atlantis*, once again in its entirety rather than in fragments, so I suspected that everything was fundamentally right with the world and decided that I wasn't yet in danger of hearing the call of Cthulhu, or scenting his reek.

After a moment or two, the noxious suggestion faded, and I got back to work again letting the train of my fanciful ideas run along the by-now well-worn track of my evolving series of tales of the biotech revolution.

I began wondering whether I might be able to make a story out of the dramatically-increased mutation-rates suffered by so-called "mammoth genes" with ten or more introns, and whether the importation of new mammoth genes to plants or animals might be used as a mechanism to speed up evolution, especially in association with artificial transposons. I posed myself the question of whether the double meaning of "mammoth" might help supply a plot as well as a title, especially if I could make out a case for prehistoric mammoths having fallen into an evolutionary trap because their own lack of mammoth genes condemned them to an inflexibility from which a dose of said supergenes might have saved them.

What might have become of the populations of pre-Ice Age Europe, I wondered, if some such dose of mutagenic potential had been provided by a comet from the Oort Cloud exploding in the atmosphere somewhere over Denmark, allowing Neanderthalers to become supermen who not only domesticated mammoths and saber-toothed tigers but became masters of mutational husbandry, pharmacogenetic alchemy and *authentic* transcendental trancing and dancing as the ice retreated and the world became Sumerland again.…

And so on.

I lost track of time, which was supposedly what I was supposed to do—but I didn't slip into an alternative state of consciousness. I remained perfectly conscious and perfectly lucid—at least to the extent that that kind of playing with ideas can qualify as lucidity.

Eventually, Axel Castle removed the two halves of the bisected ping pong ball from my face and said: ""That's excellent, Dr. Stableford. We've made all the baseline measurements—now it's a matter of analyzing them, ready for phase two tomorrow."

I wasn't entirely convinced by his judgment that the run had been "excellent." "Nothing happened," I told him. "It was just like sitting on a train, the musical leakage and occasional odd whiffs included. I was just doing what I normally do when I have dead time on my hands."

"I know," he assured me. "This is just a measuring exercise. Once we've analyzed the pattern of your brain's reflexive responses to the musical and olfactory stimuli, then we can really get cooking. Believe me, now that the machine knows the fundamental pattern of your neurological responses, it will be able to design a sequence of stimuli that will take you down through the layers of consciousness and way beyond, to a perfect somniloquent state."

"I'll look forward to it," I said, insincerely. I wasn't nearly as convinced of the infallibility of his machinery as he seemed to be.

He reached out to remove the earphones. I heard the echoes of Carl McCoy's distorted voice fading away from the contrapuntal melody, to leave the synthetic heartbeat in full possession of my earphones before they were lifted away, leaving a silence that seemed strangely obtrusive.

"Actually, I suppose I did relax a little more than usual," I told him, trying to show willing, "although I wasn't really aware of it until I came back again."

"No, you didn't," he said. ""The machines were keeping track throughout. Don't worry about it—just leave it to us. Tomorrow, the kit will be familiar to you, and we'll get a head start even before we start the hocus pocus. Then, you'll be able to get to mental states that you've never visited before, and we'll be able to see how exactly your brain reacts to our reconstructed stimuli in the somniloquent state. After that…well, everything will depend on the results we turn in, along with the application for the grant renewal. For tonight, though, you can just leave the machines to do their thing and go for a pizza."

He wasn't speaking metaphorically. Lionel and I did exactly that.

Until you've had an authentic Welsh pizza, cooked in an oven lined with authentic Pontypridd slate, topped with all the most gorgeous produce of the valleys, including nutty slack and lamb's testicles, washed down with water from the sacred Snowdonian spring that once nourished the voice of

Taliesin and the Bardic custodians of Druidic tradition, you haven't really lived....

Well, actually, I made that last bit up—all the sober reportage was getting me down, so I thought I'd relax by throwing in an improbability or two. I'll be sure to let you know if I do it again, because I have my reputation to think of—after all, what kind of writer would use himself as an unreliable narrator?

The rumor that you can order laverbread as a topping in Welsh pizza parlors is grossly exaggerated; actually, you can't—except, maybe, in Haverfordwest. What you can get in certain parts of Wales, though, on certain nights of the year, if you're really lucky, is Lionel Fanthorpe's after-dinner conversation, which is never less than hugely entertaining, even if it's only a week since you last saw him.

As in Martin's bookshop, we ran through the usual gamut of anecdotes about everyone scheduled to appear on the next series of *Fortean TV*, the plots of a significant fraction of Lionel's Badger books—except for one that he couldn't remember, which he probably hadn't actually written—and the recent exploits of his family, friends, acquaintances, and pets.

Later, the two experimenters, having done their thing, joined us again, and we went back to Axel's flat for a coffee. That was the cue for Lionel to sing a few songs, punctuated by profuse apologies for having left his guitar at home in Cardiff. It was great fun, especially watching Claire and Axel trying to get the occasional word in edgewise after Lionel had built up a—purely metaphorical—full head of steam. Had the opportunity arisen to inform them that their only hope was to rotate the word in question into the fourth dimension and then slip it back through a chronoclastic double pleat while he was drawing breath, I would have, but it never did.

On the way back to the hotel, though, I found myself in the rear seat of Claire's Hyundai with Axel.

"Did I say anything into the dictaphone while I was in the chair to-day?" I asked, because I was beginning to suspect that I might have muttered something unwittingly. I figured that the tape might be useful if I'd managed to jot down a few useful plot ideas.

"Not a word," he assured me. "That's perfectly normal, on the measuring run, although a couple of our preliminary testers did seem to feel obliged to maintain a running commentary throughout, under the impression that they were helping us out. Please don't feel obliged to start talking tomorrow, because it really doesn't make any difference so far as our reportable results are concerned. It's actually better, from our viewpoint, that the walls of consciousness separating your little ego-fragment from the Cosmic Mind didn't crack today, let alone crumble. The difference will be all the more obvious now that computer has synthesized a response to its analysis. Tomorrow is another day, as Scarlett O'Hara said to Rhett Butler."

"No she didn't," I felt obliged to tell him, for pedantic reasons. "Rhett was long gone by then. She said it to the little slave-girl—or maybe to the land itself. Well, actually, she said it to the reader…it's a writer's mission to educate his readers—or her readers, in Margaret Mitchell's case—in the utility of idiotic platitudes. It's a dark and lonely job, but somebody has to do it—just like coal-mining?"

"Not around these parts," Axel said dryly. "Not any more. Is nine o'clock in the morning too early for you?"

"No problem," I assured him, as the Hyundai pulled up outside my hotel.

"I've got to get back to Cardiff now," Lionel told me, getting out of the car briefly in order to bid me farewell. "I have to do an early-morning spot on the radio, and half a dozen other things, so I won't see you again this trip.

"Another time, then," I said. "I'm sure that Axel and Claire will let you know how it goes, as you've already made your contribution, and your results can no longer be influenced by reportage."

"I'm not sure that my session went as well as they hoped," Lionel confided, keeping his voice low, but conscientiously not going into detail.

""I've no great hopes for mine, either," I confessed. "I have difficulty relaxing at the best of times, and after my brush with Martin's bookshop last week, on top of the effects of ****'s latest desertion, I have to confess that I might be rather more wound-up than I'd like to be.

"You might try a little yoga," he suggested, ever helpful. "Perhaps it's not your skepticism that holds you back—just that you keep on thinking, long after a sensible person would have stopped for a rest, even when there's nowhere for the train of thought to go but on and on and on. Still, it was nice of you to come, and it's always good to see you."

"You too," I told him. "I'm glad you asked me. The trip won't be a total loss, even if the hypnotic computer doesn't perform the anticipated miracle. A change is as good as a rest. Do give me a ring next time you need a skeptical observer. If I'm free…."

"Will do," he promised, as he shook my hand, and then got back into the car so that Claire could drop him at the station.

I went to bed, slightly surprised to find myself as tired as I was, but looking forward to a good night's sleep.

CHAPTER XIV

The breakfast was as classy as the hotel, which is the only good thing you can say about British hotels in general. All I can ever be bothered to get for myself at home is a bowl of cereal, so it made a nice change to fill up on overstuffed sausages, crispy bacon, congealed fried eggs, slushy tomatoes and greasy fried bread. I was careful not to overdose on the coffee, though; I didn't want to get restless legs while I was sitting in the comfy chair in my hi-tech hairnet, staring into the cloudy interior of the divided ping pong ball.

I wondered briefly whether the ping pong ball that had been so cruelly sacrificed upon the Altar of Science was sufficiently in tune with the relentless surge of the Cosmic Mind to yearn for its lost wholeness, but figured that it probably wasn't. If I were a ping pong ball, I decided, I'd probably be grateful to take on the kind of work that one was now doing, even if it meant being split in two; it had to be better than being ceaselessly bashed back and forth across a table, bouncing first on this side and then on that—except when being served, in which case there would be an extra bounce accompanied by a particularly dizzying spin. What sort of existence would that be?

It would, I decided, be almost as bad as being the element in an electric kettle.

I was evidently still exceptionally light-minded—to the extent that I began to wonder whether the effects of the psychotropic dust had really worn off completely, or whether they were lingering, the way the after-effects of a cold sometimes do.

Claire's Hyundai rolled up dead on time, and Axel invited me politely to get into the front seat.

"Thanks," I said. "Okay, let's go see the Cosmic Mind. Or do I mean the Wizard of Oz? It's difficult to tell whether or not the road's made of yellow brick when there's so much grime around."

"Pontypridd is a clean town by comparison with some," Claire said, severely.

"I know," I said, although a lot of shit had flowed into the sewer since I'd last seen Bolton-on-Dearne. "I am going to give this a go, you know. I'll relax as far as I possibly can. I just can't offer any guarantees. I really don't take suggestions very easily."

"That's why we asked you to join the program," she reminded me.

The conversation lapsed then for the remainder of the drive. The two experimenters were full of nervous anticipation, and I was a trifle nervous myself, hoping, without overmuch confidence, that I could measure up to their youthful expectation.

This time, I sneaked a closer look at the odor-manufacturing equipment. One console with knobs on looks pretty much like another, and the mess of glass and plastic tubing leading to a mutant filter-funnel—which, I presumed, was where the carefully-engineered fumes came out to play in the otherwise-sterile atmosphere—looked like nothing I'd ever seen or dreamed of before, so I wasn't in any position to make productive comparisons, let alone to estimate its power or its subtlety. The synthesizer and mixer hooked up in the sound-system seemed distinctly user-friendly by comparison.

I wondered whether I might have done better to bring *Bringing It All Back Home*, so that I could go dancing with *Mr. Tambourine Man* and investigate the *Gates of Eden*, but figured that another trip to Lost Atlantis would probably do almost as well, and that if "Last Exit for the Lost" couldn't take me out of myself and into the dark underbelly of the mind, nothing was ever likely to.

"Okay?" Axel said, as he covered my eyes.

"Peachy," I assured him. "As a matter of interest, will the drug-addled lap-dancer make the team for the six-month tour, if you get the funding?"

"Oh yes," he said. "She might have been born for trancing: a natural. Going beyond bliss is child's play for her. We have high hopes."

"That doesn't exactly fill one with confidence about the Cosmic Mind's IQ, does it?" I sniped. "It doesn't make one keen to snuggle up in the universal bosom, either. Imagine how disappointing it would be to get in touch with the Ultimate only to find that the entire universe has a bad case of Alzheimer's Entropy complicated by Spiritual Syphilis."

"Imagine how much it will appreciate your input, then," Axel murmured. "Are you ready for the big beat?"

I was.

As Axel had shrewdly pointed out, the day before, I was used to the apparatus now. It's amazing how quickly repetition can turn into ritual, how casually one can discard a reflexive sense of unease. It was only the second time I'd sat in the comfy chair, but it already seemed perfectly familiar; as soon as the fake heartbeat got into its measured stride I had the sensation of recovering something whose absence, although unnoticed, had been troubling me at some subliminal level.

Let's see, I thought. *Where was I, exactly...?*

For at least ten thousand years, I reminded myself, mental and social evolution had outstripped the physiological evolution of a body whose emotional equipment was shaped by brutality. In the future of genetic engineering, however, I assumed that physiological evolution would far outstrip the mental and social evolution of a brain whose moral equipment had been shaped by terror. When that process really began to get into gear, I thought, the evolution and metamorphosis of the dark mind, and the kind of pact forged between the Faustian Age and its resident Devil might really begin to pay dividends, on either side.

That was the world, I thought, for which the modern mind ought to be preparing itself, and it probably needed all the help it could get, especially from science fiction…and that, I thought, was why I probably wasn't wasting my time while I sat in the midst of that mock-Frankensteinian set-up. Not that I had any illusions, even then, about the likelihood of my own science fiction being able to influence anyone's thinking, in spite of the occasional propagandistic fervor that I put into it. I knew only too well that my work wasn't popular, and never would be, partly because of my stubborn determination not to pander to the kind of reader expectations that I'd intended to discuss with the Devil before I found that he wasn't interested in that sort of intellectual discussion.

I didn't realize in 1997, of course, how fast the decline was going to be, not only of my own ever-precarious career as I was relegated permanently from the commercial sector but of publishing as a whole and generic science fiction in particular. I knew which way the compass needle was pointing, though,. Even so, I thought at the time, intellectually-stimulating science fiction still had a potential role to play, for the few people who still liked it and were prepared to read it, in helping as-yet-unblown minds to adapt to the mind-blowing possibilities of the future, and it was surely the duty of every conscientious science fiction writer to do his bit, even if he ended up—as, in fact, I have—working in a virtual vacuum.

So, with reference to the project in hand and my second session in the chair, I figured that even if there was no possibility of my actually slipping into a trance state, let alone of going beyond bliss into the uncharted realms of the unconscious, there was a sense in which I was fully entitled to think that I might be more closely in touch with the heartbeat and muscle of the Cosmos, and the evolution of its dark mind, than any hallucinogen-soaked and endorphin-drenched trance-and-dancer was ever likely to be.

So, at least, I surely had to believe, if I were to continue to take myself seriously, or even if I were to continue to think of my babbling-brook-of-consciousness as a tale worth retailing, a narrative worth reviewing, a seam worth seeming and a source of enlightenment worth trading with the Devil.

Whether there was, in fact, a Cosmic Mind or not—and whether, if so, one could meet it without dissolving into a puddle of Lovecraftian *angst*—there was still work to be done in picking away at the coal-face of the futuristic imagination, hewing fuel for the fires of the intellect that would burn brighter, in spite of its blackness, than any heap of twigs amassed by a curious ape on the African plain…or, for that matter, any pitiless Jurassic sun, whose reptile-favoring glare never dreamed of eclipse…or even any submarine volcanic flux stirring the primal mud into the first repetitive semblances of life.…

However comfortable I might eventually become in the seductive arms of Axel Castle's mind-blowing kit, I figured that I needed to continue working in the meantime… to plan…to plot…to carry through my tiny part in the great diabolical pact, trying to do my bit for the enlightenment of the unconscious.

I didn't expect, for a moment, actually to get to where Axel and Claire wanted to send me, but I figured that it didn't really matter, because I had to do the relevant work from wherever I stood and wherever I might be able to stand.

Oddly enough, though, the kinds of plot that them began to come drifting into my mind, as I did my honest best to play the game, and relax to the point at which Axel and Claire might think that they'd got their fifty quid's worth out of me, weren't the same kinds of plots that had drifted into my mind the previous day. Those had been science fiction plots, extrapolating ideas that were at least on the margins of rational plausibility: ideas with a modicum of scrupulous logical sensitivity.

I tried to focus on such ideas again—especially the idea of the bi-opiracy story, because I was sure that it was an idea of which I might be able to make something if only I could get a narrative handle on it—but I couldn't. For some reason, my mind kept slipping away from that kind of quasi-scientific thinking, reaching for a more primitive lexicon of ideas,

The notions that began to rise up from the unconscious for aesthetic appraisal when Axel and Claire began to feed the results of the computer analysis of my psyche into the music track that was playing in my earphones, with periodic olfactory stimulation and provocation, were motifs of another and more intellectually anarchic kind, plunging me directly into the surreal and the absurd.

I thought about Biggles, in his earliest incarnation as a pilot in World War I, taking his Sopwith Camel into a weird cloud while being chased by Spads on night patrol, and being temporarily displaced into a marginal nightmarish dimension, where the exhaust fumes of his engine begin to take on demonic form, attempting to gain some kind of substance, to become living smoke, as the first step on a magical metamorphic ladder that might eventually pave the way for an invasion of the human realm by predatory vaporous monsters....

The narrative advantage of stories like that, of course, as I'd planned to explain to the Devil before he cut me off, is that they have their endings already built-in. On the previous day, I'd had difficulty carrying any of my ideas through to anything that looked like a respectable narrative closure, because the trouble with futuristic fiction is that the future never ends, being fully occupied in eternal processes of beginning and becoming. Fantasy, light or dark, is very different; fantasy is always end-orientated, always the produce of wishes and fears, always aimed at fulfillment or escape, and the writer's job is merely to organize a pleasing trajectory or an ingenious obstacle course to delay the inevitable consummation.

On the other hand, given my principles of narrative subversion, I couldn't be content with the inbuilt narrative strategies; I knew that I had to work for their perversion. I couldn't relax my writer's conscience to the extent of letting formula rule.

All that Biggles has to do, in the fictional world of conventional expectation, is to fly out of the cloud again, to return to the bright and bitter normality of the Spad-filled skies, and then land safely on the ground. A conventional nightmare, however nasty, only has to be dispelled, even if its menacing motif is careful to leave disturbing a hint behind to remind the characters and the reader that the threat of dissolution is still there and always will be. Nowadays, you aren't allowed to accomplish that fictive sleight-of-hand that by having your protagonist wake up to the discovery that he's been asleep, but there are various of ways of achieving the transition deceptively...and it's always there, drawing the tale like a lodestone the size of the Earth.

My problem, therefore, seen as a means of developing what was, in any case, a fairly silly idea, was to find some way for the evolution of the metamorphic exhaust within the cloud to become something that could not simply be put away and banished, but something that would begin a transformation of the world within the text, in spite of the fact that history and the literary development of Biggles' later career were equally unaware of any such transformation....

I could smell something, but it wasn't the savannah.

I couldn't quite make it out, but I didn't know whether its enigmatic quality was subjective or objective. It was non-invasive, Axel had promised, and completely harmless, so it couldn't be ether or chloroform or anything that was going to send me to the Land of Dreams, even in combination with a saraband for dead lovers or an excursion to Bosch's Garden of Delight—which is, after all, the world as it is, colored by the human imagination, safely set aside from heaven and hell.

It was probably the effect of my allergy, I thought, that was preventing me recognizing the odor, although I doubted that it would evoke a memory even if I had the nose of a hungry hyena.

Then I thought about a musician, perhaps a composer, perhaps half of some Gothic duo, who acquires an elusive stalker, perhaps glimpsing some female figure in black who always disappears in the shadows, but who also manifests herself in enigmatic e-mails and cryptic answerphone messages, who might be some kind of vampiric muse or, more promisingly, some kind of bizarre melomaniac creature instinctively attracted by his work, and with whom he becomes obsessed in either case, unable to shake the idea that he might be able to gift her the extra substance she lacks and so fervently desires, if only at cost of his own....

That story too, and all its routine variants, had its conventional ending built in. The musician/composer/painter/writer has to die, of course, after the long fade to grey, exhausting himself in his futile quest for the unattainable and thus abstracting himself from a world in which he doesn't really belong, from which he is dispelled in spite of having to do it by being spelled, correctly or not, in a world where enchantment is given a poetic license to work...that being, of course, the very nature of fantasy....

At least, I thought, that kind of tragic ending can't qualify as uplifting, and in spite of its repetitive quality, it has a capacity to disturb, which only needs a certain stylistic deftness to being out a sufficiently distinctive strangeness....

The sound feeding through my earphones was unfamiliar now, albeit in a generic sort of way. The Gothic quality was still there, and the synthesizers were still producing recognizable rhythms, although there were no vocals, but the melodies seemed to be strangely intrusive and strangely suggestive.

I began to feel a kind of prickling sensation in my limbs, which I recognized as a symptom of sitting for too long in the same position, although it didn't evaporate when I moved imperceptibly within the chair.

I began once again to wonder, more earnestly and more anxiously, whether the effects of the fungus had worn off as completely as I'd assumed, or even whether the sterling work done by my immune system in cleansing my blood had nevertheless left islands of infection somewhere. If it had, I supposed, further viral eruptions might begun at any moment, bring the Devil back into my life, not necessarily as a material presence and a visual image, but perhaps as a subtler, largely invisible and intangible entity, perhaps no longer capable of telling stories or asking questions but nevertheless capable of negotiating and extending pacts....

But I dismissed that thought, as essentially unhelpful, and I returned to thinking about potential stories.

Yet again, my mind seemed to shy away from the possibilities of bio-technology, drawn by some exotic psychological magnetism to work in a more primitive vein, with a darker and cruder system of ideas. It didn't matter; I was a writer, and versatile, I could deal with any kind of imaginative raw material. The essential thing was to keep control of it, always to keep the potential story in mind, and to try to import a little originality into it, as well as a little calculated perversity.

I thought about the possibility that a nineteenth century whore might begin to think that she can see the fairy folk as her syphilis develops into its tertiary, mind-rotting phase, and convinces herself by slow degrees that she is the rightful Queen of Elfland...which would not necessarily an attractive prospect, if Faerie Queens only reign for a single day before being ritually sacrificed and their blood scattered on the fields where various kinds of forbidden fruit are carefully cultivated...except that the restriction might not be as inconvenient as all that, because a day in Faerie could be equivalent to seven years on Earth and might last every bit as long, subjectively speaking, provided that the faeries can always hear elfin music playing...which would be easy enough to contrive, if the elfin fiddlers could be forced by magic to keep on playing and the elfin rhymers to keep on singing and the dancers to keep on and on and on....

Stories like that have perfectly natural endings too, because they have a fixed span built into them from the very beginning, which only has to run its allotted course, like fate, or destiny, or a chapter-by-chapter plan roughed out on the back of an old envelope. The hallucinating whore has to die, of course, because that's what syphilis eventually does to whores, but that's not the point of that kind of story, which is that the brute facts of vicious reality needn't matter to you if you have a way to get around them. If, by means of one narrative device or another, or simply a surreal transition, you can slip into the nth dimension, and fly edgewise as far away from the world as wings of desire can take you, even if you know that sooner or later you'll flutter into a chronofantastic whirlpool and come bouncing back into the world, spinning like mad, to resume the game of serve-smash-and-bounce, serve-smash-and-bounce....

By that time, I thought I could see something inside the blinkers, but I knew that it was only something within my eyes, like hypnagogic or hypnopompic imagery, or phosphenes, or...was that tune really one of mine, or any kind of derivative thereof, or had Axel or Claire slipped in something of his or her own? And what was that musty smell, reeking of damp and the dark? Was it air captured in a deep coal-mine, or fungus imprisoned in the pages of an old book? Might it be something scraped from the inner brickwork of a dynamited chimney, or liquid life dredged from the depths of glutinous soil? Might it be cyanobacteria or urschleim dredged from the utmost depths of the marine abyss, from the lip of a black smoker?

I shook my hands, and that seemed to get rid of the pins and needles, at least temporarily. For the first time I wondered how long I had been in the chair, and how much longer the experiment had to run.

This time, I was sure that I hadn't said a word into the dictaphone so far, and I hadn't wanted to, because I didn't have anything to say, but I began to wonder whether I ought to make the effort, if only for my own sake, in order to stay focused, and to help myself to make the most of the plots that were becoming increasingly difficult to negotiate, given my reluctance simply to accept the conventional formulae and relax into mere narrative ritual.

The discomfort really wasn't bad enough, as yet, to be worth issuing a complaint.

So, I thought about making up a story about making a deal with a demon, which would obviously be quite different from my actual experience of making such a deal, which was still too fresh in memory to be readily fictionalized, but which would nevertheless involve a deft symbolization of the Faustian Age and the human predicament therein, given the current phase of the evolution of the collective unconscious.

I thought about inventing a hypothetical deal made under inconvenient circumstances, because Satan is dead as a result of a second war in Heaven, and the demon in the story has become a refugee from a devastated Hell, no longer having any real interest in human souls, although he might be willing to trade a few magical favors for a share of the summoner's bodily experience—to which the narrator of the story will naturally agree, because that's the kind of guy he is, with the result that while in possession of him, the demon can confer a visionary talent on his summoner, which has a permanent effect far outlasting the culmination of the deal, and which renders the aforementioned magical favors redundant by overwriting all the appetites that they might have served....

That's the kind of conclusion that qualifies as an ironic twist in stories of that sort, which always end in ironic twists because that's the kind of story they are, there not being much call for demons in straightforward horror stories any more, since TV overkill reduced them all to the status of infusoria-ex-machina, although all horror eventually turns into comedy anyhow, because that's what a sense of humor is for, if you think about it... which you really ought to, even if it doesn't look like a useful source of new plots, because there has to be more to life than work, after all, if there's any sense in which a writer can ever stop working, which there probably isn't....

The discomfort was increasing, but I knew what it was. It *was* an after-effect of the psychotropic fungus that had allowed me to meet the Devil, but it wasn't just a relapse or a recurrence. During its sojourn in my body and its hard-fought war against my immune system, I thought, the fungus must have actually mutated and gone through a crucial gateway in the process of natural selection, which had produced descendants that were benign in a better sense than the conventional way of talking about cancers, which just meant that they didn't do much harm, but in the sense of being genuinely benign, potentially capable of entering into a symbiotic relationship with the body and the mind alike, or at least with their dark components....

It would be foolish, of course, I told myself. to think of the mutated fungus as a demon, or any other minion of the Devil, and just as foolish to think of it as an emissary of the Cosmic Mind, but even so, it would surely be something more than a mere magic mushroom....

At any rate, the discomfort I felt wasn't threatening in any way. It wasn't nausea or a fever, or even an intoxication. It was, I assured myself, just a process of mutual adaptation.

Or maybe, I thought, the demon story could avoid the bathetic twist, and put on a cloak of metaphysical pretension, developing the notion that there's something profound in the idea of a reconfigured cosmos in which Heaven and Hell are obsolete and a whole new metaphysical "superstructure" is in the making, reflecting the changing pattern of human understanding, anxiety and yearning, in which everything would eventually be reconfigured in exactly the progressive fashion that my own diabolical pact had envisioned.

That would include, of course, the dark mental substance of the Cosmic Mind, which wouldn't be subdivided on any crude Freudian lines into a deistic superego and a diabolical id, or any mere set of quasi-Jungian archetypes, but would be something more along the lines of the kind of sentient Cosmos that might be conceivable in a scientific world-view: a universal mentality that can dream of such things as the implicate order, the quantum theory of the will, the Omega Point, the inflationary universe and all the lovely jargon of quarks and beauty, strangeness and charm... because, after all, truth is strangeness and charm as well as beauty, and we really do need to know that, even if we haven't quite brought that knowledge to the surface of consciousness as yet....

Which is, when you think about it, I told myself, while being careful not to say so aloud, *is what all this narrative questing really ought to be about. Eternity's Eve...yet another chance to deploy a title you've been trying to fit a story to for years. A universe infinitely replicating itself as the Cosmic Mind searches for an original idea, a story that doesn't have its ending ready built-in, while memory leakage re-acquaints the favored children of eternity with their former lives and former mistakes and makes them dream of trance and dance and transcendence and all their echoes in out-of-body experiences, flight and cosmic voyages through space and time....*

...and worlds in which the dead are afraid of coming to life again and losing the refined, sensitive emotional spectrum of infection by love and greed, pain and joy, and all the other afflictions of the tumorous flesh that grows like mould upon their bones while existential angst caused by the terror of life runs riot in their utterly sane and rational minds....

...and plagues of bookworms devour the ink of diaries and registers of birth and death, newspapers and financial accounts, junk mail and parlia-mentary reports, excreting it all as an infinite epic poem whose lines surge and swell to the rhythm of the spheres, telling tales of all the heroes there ever were, and all the accomplishments they ever made on behalf of all the folks back home, that being what heroes are and what heroes do, whose stories never, ever end....

The music had ceased—or, to be strictly accurate, I had ceased to hear it. I could still smell something, though, very faintly; at first I thought it might be incense, but then I figured out that it was just burning.

But there is no Hell, I reminded myself. *I know that for a fact, because the Devil told me so himself, and he isn't the Father of Lies, but an honest broker, striving for enlightenment and willing to barter for it, idea for idea, insight for insight and paradox for paradox, because he is, at the end of the day, a storyteller and a story, a narrative device invented by consciousness in order to begun the work of trying to make sense of the unconscious and the dark mentality composing it.*

And that was when I began to think about the Cosmic Mind: not to see it, because, being the antithesis of the Devil, it isn't the kind of entity that can ever be seen; and not to hear it, because although it's the ultimate source of all harmony, it isn't music itself, and although its very essence in the Word it has no voice; but just to think about it and to try and fit it into a plot, and thus to make contact with it in the only way that any light mind can, by searching the darkness for inspiration and imagination, for suggestion and for something...perhaps the hint or root of an odor...that might be on the threshold of emergence, of dark mind becoming light, of unconsciousness becoming conscious....

"The Cosmic Mind, when you really think about it," I said to Alex and Claire, aloud, "is more ancient than the stars whose dust we are, and yet it's young...so very young, so very ambitious, so magnificently and triumphantly dead that it need never fear any return to meager life, nor any conclusive extinction while it has the power to form a single thought...that thought being, according to tradition, *fiat lux*, except that the author of that particular scriptural passage probably misheard what was being dictated to him, which was in fact *fiat luxe*, the Cosmic Mind knowing all languages and not being afraid of any miscegenation, any more than it could ever be content with mere light when it could have luxury instead....

"...and what *is* a universe, after all, but luxury incarnate, especially a universe minded to contain life as well as light, so fertile with its power of invention as to imagine the ascent of the *urschleim* to cyanobacterial effervescence and then to the tree of life, on a tide of *élan vital*, ultimately to become to be the kind of being who is sufficiently fond of himself—or herself—to imagine that getting back in touch with the Cosmic Mind might be an experience as rewarding as an acid trip, or a lap dance, or a combination of the two, when anyone with half a brain or half a ping pong ball can smell and see the obvious conclusion that we ought not to be content with tales with obvious conclusions, which lead inexorably to fulfillments or escapes, when what we ought to be concerned with is an infinitude of beginnings and becomings and making ourselves more human than we already are, more divided than we already are, more separate and secluded and busy and immune to boredom than we already are....

"...because, when you think about it, anyone who actually could go beyond the bliss state to bathe in the all-encompassing climax of the Cosmic Mind would have reached a conclusion to which there was no conceivable sequel, a punctuation mark which permitted no continuation, a completeness whose aesthetic neatness would be tantamount to annihilation, beyond comedy or tragedy, *lux* or *luxe* or lucks or looks...beyond even Wordplay—which is to say, a return to the Void....

"...and that wouldn't be acceptable, would it, not just because it's nihilistic but simply because it is an ending, in a universe that ought to be all beginnings, all new possibilities, all strange twists, subversions and perversions, and never vanity or vexation of spirit, or frustration at something finished that can't be remade, which has no light or luxury or lust....

"...so no, in sum, I don't want to touch the Cosmic Mind, or to be touched by it; I want to let it alone, no matter how fearful its loneliness might be, and I want at least the possibility of making and remaking my own contacts with material and immaterial things...."

I could have gone on. I always can...but I had to stop then.

I could smell blood. Nor was it a smell that Axel's machine as feeding me, although it wasn't exactly real either, but mere like the metaphorical blood of my own severed head, soaking my own imaginary cravat, the nourishment and evidence of my own ghoulishness.

Which was not, as it turned out, a good thing, at least from the point of view of the experimenters who were paying me, although not very well, for my not-very-valuable time.

CHAPTER XV

"Did you get all that?" I asked Axel.

"Every word," he said. He sounded less than delighted.

"Well?"

"It's not exactly what we're looking for," said Axel.

I was dumbfounded. I couldn't imagine what he meant. So far as I could see, I'd been an ideal subject. In what way could I possibly have failed? I had actually done it; I really had made contact with the dark mind, facilitating its eruption into the brightness of consciousness.

"I suppose it's possible," said Axel, after a glance at Claire Louchon that testified very clearly to the fact that she didn't expect any such thing, "that you're trying to help, but to be honest, you're not. Results like that are only going to make the whole thing look like a sham."

"But...." I stopped. Words, for once, failed me.

"We know," said Claire Louchon, coldly. "You can drop the act."

"*What* do you know?" I snapped.

"We have the machine, Dr. Stableford," Axel said, wearily and perhaps sadly. "It doesn't lie. It turns out that you were right—you're absolutely immune even to the kinds of hypnosis at our disposal. Your brain activity never dropped below the level of active consciousness for a second. You were alert for every minute of the last three hours. That monologue, while not without a certain bizarre charm, never really sounded like authentic somniloquence. It was just...well, it was just *storytelling*."

I looked at the pair of them as if they were mad.

They were accusing me of making the whole thing up!

In a sense, obviously, they were right—but how could they possibly think that there wasn't a sense in which all their other subjects, past and future, weren't "making it up" too?

"But I did what you wanted me to do!" I complained. I almost added that I'd played the game seriously, but stopped when I realized that, from their viewpoint, that would give entirely the wrong impression.

I was tempted to accuse them of scientific dishonesty: of making up their minds in advance what they wanted to find, and then discarding any data that didn't fit their preconceived notions. I was also tempted to tell them that if they weren't prepared to accept the results they got, their great experiment was doomed to failure, not just in the true sense that they wouldn't discover anything, but in the increasingly important pragmatic sense that they wouldn't have a cat in hell's chance of getting a continuation of their funding—which was a pity, I thought, because crude as it was, the basic idea of what they were trying to accomplish was certainly intriguing.

I resisted both temptations. For one thing, there was no point. For another, they were young, and wouldn't have listened. And to cap it all, I really did feel a trifle guilty that I'd disappointed them, even though I didn't think that it was my fault, and because I really had played the game with the utmost seriousness.

I blinked. Claire had turned up the dimmed lights, a trifle abruptly, and my eyes were still fresh out of the ping pong balls. The earphones had been taken off and laid aside, but somewhere in the distance I could hear Artaud Franzmann wailing about *Necromanteion*, so faintly that the words could hardly penetrate the thunderous pulse of the world whose melody they were trying so plaintively to provide.

Then that was gone too. So had the hair-net.

I had been right after all. My head was too hard. I was never going to get to the hypothetical bliss state, let alone beyond it. My brain just couldn't let go of consciousness, even while I was making deals with the Devil and making mental contact with the Cosmic Mind.

The experimenters shouldn't have been disappointed, of course. A dutiful experimenter shouldn't make up his mind in advance what he's going to find, even if he has to find it in order to get his research grant extended. And a dutiful experimenter shouldn't fall in love with his own program to the extent that he imagines that it's infallible. No true scientist should ever bet the Devil his heart, because science is all about betting your head, and you have to be a serious student of possibility if you're going to win that kind of bet.

But still, I couldn't help feeling guilty as I observed their disappointment, as if I'd somehow broken the pact I'd made with them in agreeing to take part in their experimental run.

It really wasn't my fault, but I felt responsible anyway.

"I'm sorry," I said to Axel, meekly. There was nothing really to add to that, but he didn't reply, so I had no alternative but to fill the silence with levity. "I guess that bliss simply isn't for me," I said. "As for what might lie beyond bliss…well, we'll just have to leave that to the lap-dancers and members of the SPR, won't we? Let's hope that your other subjects come up with the goods."

"There's only one lap-dancer," he told me, slightly absent-mindedly, "and it's just a hobby." He didn't specify the number of members of the SPR they had lined up, although I knew that there was at least one.

"Why could I smell blood?" I asked, looking round and suddenly remembered why I'd called a sudden halt to my communion with the Cosmic Mind. I looked suspiciously at the olfactory synthesizer, as anyone would.

"What do you mean?" asked Claire. "When?"

I was already fairly sure that it hadn't been them or their machine that had fed me the sensation, but I was grateful nevertheless for the confirmation. Perhaps, I thought, it had been the Devil, or the ghost of Fred West—it certainly wasn't the sort of thing that the Cosmic Mind would do—but I knew, even as I formed the thought, that it was my own cravat.

I picked up a scalpel from the bench and split Axel's skull in two like a fractured ping pong ball, with a single dexterous sweep of my right hand. There was blood everywhere, and the blood was green. As the mask of flesh dissolved, I saw the alien creature within the human shell: the unspeakable compound of all things loathsome. It could have been a shoggoth, but how was I to know? Claire screamed, and then dropped dead, the life having been frightened right out of her. Psychologists are so impressionable.

Well, no, I made that bit up, because I felt that the story might benefit from a little melodramatic violence. In reality, I'm not the violent type. I wasn't straining under the awful yoke of sober reportage and longing to be free; I just thought that the story might gain from a hint of a flamboyant climax, and a surprise ending. As the actual pattern of happenstance had failed dismally to provide one, as it so often does, I felt that I ought to step in. Some readers like that sort of thing. If you're one of them, you might as well stop now, forget that you started reading the present paragraph and don't read any more. Hold on to the idea of the shoggoth, and everything going to hell, or to the image of the hero bravely gripping his *deus ex machina*, having saved the world from the invention that food science was not meant to know...whichever suits you best.

The rest of the actual story is, I fear, far too plausible for its own good.

"So I didn't make the team for the long haul," I said to the world-weary experimentalist. "There'll be no recall for the skiffy writer."

"Don't be too disappointed," Axel said. "We'll find a skeptic somewhere whose brain isn't quite as set in its ways as yours. Lionel gave us a few more names. I'll write you a check for your fee, but you'll have to give me a receipt."

It wasn't quite as dispiriting as the time I got invited to dinner with the government's chief scientific adviser and had to turn him down because I was teaching in Winchester on the evening in question, but it was close. It shouldn't have been; after all, not having to take part in the long-term program would save me a lot of time and a certain amount of hassle, and might even guarantee that I would never see Pontypridd again as long as I lived....

But even so....

"Given another hour or so," I told the terrible two, while Claire drove me back to the station and I sat in the back on my own because Alex had taken the front seat, in Lionel's absence, "I think I might have come up with a few usable plot ideas. Which reminds me—if you're not going to use the Dictaphone tape, can I have it, or at least get a copy? Even if there's nothing in it you can use, there might be something I can reprocess."

"Of course," said Axel. "I'll send you a copy."

"I don't think there's anything useful on it, though," Claire told me, witheringly. "It's just drivel. You must have been very bored."

"I don't get bored," I told her, severely. "I'm a writer." I looked out of the side window to emphasize my ability to transcend unpromising circumstance.

Somehow, the abandoned pitheads seemed more poignant now than they had before, and the thought of those lonely seams of unappreciated anthracite, buried deeper than bliss, was almost too much to bear.

"Maybe that's the problem, Dr. Stableford," Axel chirped up from the back of the Hyundai. "Your mind just stays busy, even when it's locked away on its own."

Claire Louchon had to have the last word. She looked at me through her blue-tinted spectacles as my train came in and said: "The trouble with you, Dr. Stableford, is that you're too self-contained. You need to learn to let go."

"Amen to that," I said, insincerely, while thinking precisely the opposite.

CHAPTER XVI

It couldn't end there, of course. Even if that had been the sum total of what happened, the story couldn't end there, because then it would simply be an instance of exactly the kind of story that runs counter to my principles: the kind where some disruptive element of fantasy comes along to interfere with the course of normal life, and then is simply canceled out and annihilated, so that the world can return to its tedious course, undisturbed in any meaningful or significant way.

Except, of course, that there's a sense in which it *did* have to end that way, because all of this happened in 1997, and nearly twenty years of history have happened since then, and nothing has been disrupted in any meaningful or significant way, in the general way of the world or in the pattern of my own personal existence. So, there's a sense in which the present story isn't able to escape its normalizing ending, no matter how much I might want to avoid it, for esthetic reasons—unless, of course, there's some ingenious method of having it both ways, of having the appearance of normality restored, while at least dropping heavy hints that the annihilation of the disturbing factor wasn't complete, that behind the apparent restoration, behind that thin crust of reality on which we all skate, safely contained and nurtured by the limitations of everyday consciousness, something actually had changed, permanently.

And, unsurprisingly, for anyone who believes that the He, or the Cosmic Mind, has an atom of esthetic sensibility—and how can we not, when we consider seriously the beauty, strangeness and charm of the world as it is, let alone the gorgeous multiplicity of imagined worlds that we can invent?—that's the way it actually worked out in 1997, and how it has worked out today.

When the train from Pontypridd got into Cardiff, where I was due to catch a connection back to Reading, home, normality and the everyday labor of making up fanciful stories, I decided, instead, to hope on a train to Barry, to go and visit Martin's bookshop again, since I had Lionel's assurance that he hadn't actually burned the books from Glofeydd Diafol—at least, not yet.

I didn't have any fully-formed intention of exposing myself for a second time to the mysterious fungus, not because I didn't want to meet the Devil again or renew my slight acquaintance with Him, in the hope of getting to know Him a little bit better, but because I didn't want to spend another two days in bed feeling like shit in the purgatorial interim between the two. But what I did have a firm intention of doing was to fill the two plastic bags that I always carried with me in those days for routine book-hunting purposes with books: books whose printed contents might be devoid of all interest, but might still have the Devil between the lines.

I hadn't really thought the matter through beyond the acquisition of the books. I didn't have any plan for taking them to the microbiology or biochemistry labs at Reading University and asking someone to mount a search for the relevant spores and a chemical assay of any psychotropic alkaloids they might contain. I certainly hadn't thought of contacting any pharmaceutical company with a view to any kind of eventual economic development, whether as a "legal" high or for some medical purpose yet to be discovered. My first instinct was basically that of the book-accumulator, wanting to make sure that something unusual was preserved, even if it simply continued to exist, in the way it had while the remnants of the library had been sitting in the boxes that Martin had eventually bought.

I had no intention of disturbing my normality more than that. I just wanted to exclude the possibility of going through the rest of my life regretting the fact that I'd missed an opportunity to fill a hole in my collection. I didn't want Martin's bookshop to become akin to the bookshops of my dreams, its potential lost forever no matter how many times I returned to it in sleep, with all the nostalgia of *déjà-vu*.

When I got to the shop, however, I found that I was too late.

Two men in brown overalls, wearing heavy-duty smog masks, were just loading the last of a brand new set of hermetically-sealed boxes into the back of an unmarked white van, under the watchful eye of Penny from the SPR—or, I immediately deduced, in his particular instance, Penny from the Awdurdod Datblygu Cymru.

She seemed a trifle surprised, and not by any means delighted, to see me, but there was a sight gleam of triumph in her eye as she took note of my evident disappointment at having been forestalled.

"Mr. Stableford," he said, in her musical Welsh lilt. "I didn't expect to see you here. Martin didn't mention that you'd be coming back."

"It was a spur of the moment thing," I said. "I was in Cardiff changing trains and I thought, *why not?* It's a common book collector thing—you visit a shop, and you hesitate over something, decide to leave it, and then spend the next week wishing you hadn't, until you simply have to go back and get it…if you can."

"I'm sorry," she said, not sounding in the least sorry, "but you're too late. Nothing I can do about it, if fear. It's out of my hands: a health and safety issue. Martin contacted us, you see, after he's spent another two days feeling ill, having deciding that you were right all along: that his shop wasn't haunted and didn't need exorcising, but that it did need a very thorough cleaning."

While she was speaking, the first white van drew away, and a second drew up to park in exactly the same spot, with quasi-military precision. Two more men dressed in identical overalls, wearing identical heavy-duty smog-masks, leapt out, opened up the back and started unloading equally heavy-duty industrial cleaning equipment.

"And this is a service that the ADC provides, is it?" I asked, skeptically.

She actually linked arms with me then, and drew me away down the street, in the direction of the sea—or, to be strictly accurate, the Bristol Channel.

"I don't know you very well, Mr. Stableford," she said, "but I have a shrewd suspicion of the kind of thinking that might be going on in your highly imaginative brain at the moment. Did Lionel tell you that I spent the weekend up the valleys, looking for ghosts on behalf of the SPR?"

"Yes, he did," I said. "And until approximately three minutes ago, I believed him."

"But now you suspect that I was there on ADC business?"

"Health and Safey issues, perhaps," I suggested. I had already decided that I ought not, on any account, to mention the dreaded word Taffia.

"That's what it is," she said, blandly, "as I think you know very well. After all, you got an even bigger dose of the stuff than poor Martin, even though you tried hard to minimize your account of the effects when I phoned you. I could tell that you were hiding something, you know."

"How?" I asked curiously. She hadn't got a larger dose than Lionel, so far as I know. Even though she'd felt queasy enough to phone me—or so she'd said—she couldn't have absorbed enough to cause hallucinations. She shouldn't have had any reason to think that I was hiding anything.

"When you suggested that there might be something in the books that was causing Martin's conviction that the shop was haunted, with the associated physical symptoms, to you it was just one more idea to toy with and thrown out," she said, "but I took it seriously. That's why I asked someone to nip round there on Tuesday to collect some samples and get someone in the SCS lab to take a look, in case there was a serious Health and Safety issue."

"SCS?" I queried.

"Scientific Civil Service," she told me. Apparently the Cardiff division didn't make a fetish out of having its own Welsh-language acronym after the fashion if the WDA/ADC.

"And they managed not only to submit a report but to get an actual operation off the ground within a week?" I said. "By Civil Service standards, that's greased lightning."

"To tell you the truth, Mr. Stableford, "she said, when we reached the shore, "I'd appreciate it, since you're here, if you'd come in for a medical check-up, and I'd also be grateful if you'd be willing to give me a fuller account of any hallucinations that you might have suffered during the last few days."

I was still mulling that over with regard to my well-developed medical phobias, and thinking about the best way to couch my flat refusal when the truly significant word she's used, perhaps because of a slip of the tongue but more probably because she wanted me to know that she knew.

"What do you mean, *fuller*?" I said, sharply.

"Just a manner of speaking," she said, her lilt still melodious and perfectly even, without the slightest hint of embarrassment. "I meant, any account at all, of any psychotropic symptoms you might have suffered."

I hadn't told her, or given her any reason to think, that I might have suffered any hallucinogenic symptoms at all. There was only one person who could have given her any indication that I might, and he'd dismissed the evidence in question as something utterly and completely insignificant. Maybe he'd meant it—but the fact remained that Axel Castle had talked to Penny from the ADC before he'd subjected me to his psyche-diving kit, and he must have phoned her afterwards—immediately afterwards—to tell her what he'd found. So much for the ethics of confidentiality and the necessity of not influencing the expectations of his other subjects.

He wasn't even Welsh.

That had to be it, I knew, or part of it. From the point of view of the English, Wales is just an eccentric extension of England—or was, back in 1997, before devolution constructed a Welsh Government of sorts—but the stalwarts of the Welsh Development Agency didn't see it the same way. Almost by definition, they were a competitive organization, looking after specifically Welsh interests, in opposition to English ones.

I actually laughed.

"What's funny?" she asked.

"You're actually scared of English biopiracy," I said. "You're genuinely worried about the possibility of English biotech buccaneers moving in to usurp the possible Eldorado of Glofeydd Diafol."

"And you think that's funny, do you?" she said, mildly. Evidently, she didn't—and there was a sense, I suppose, in which she was probably right.

"I gather that you're not going to tell me what your SCS analyst found in the samples you took from Martin's shop last week?" I said, "let alone what you hope to find in those boxes your white van took away."

"Of course not," she said. "It's really none of your business."

I couldn't agree with that, but I could see a certain fairness in it. After all, I wasn't going to accept her invitation to a free medical check-up, and I wasn't ready yet to give her a full account of my pact with the Devil.

I had options, of course. I could tip Lionel off about what was going on, given that Penny presumably had to intention of giving him any hard information either, but there was no point. Even if *Fortean TV* or the *Fortean Times* decided to do a story on WDA cover-ups and Taffia conspiracy theories, and the possible dark secrets still lurking beneath the slagheaps of Glofeydd Diafol, nobody would believe a word of it. It would just be a joke.

And I knew that if I tried to tell the story myself, to anyone, it would just be a story, just a fantasy, just another item of absurdist science fiction—because that's what I do. That's what I am.

And in any case, in the interests of simple justice, wasn't Penny from the ADC right in wanting to keep the possible rewards of any discovery that might be made in the ruins of Pwllmerys at home, safe from the avid hands of English biopiracy? What right did I, as a Yorkshireman, have to interfere, especially as we tend to look askance at anyone hailing from south of Doncaster or the far side of the Pennines, just as the true Welsh naturally loathe and distrust the English in general?

What I asked myself, would the Devil advise me to do? Or, more pertinently, what would I advise the Devil to do, in pursuance of the terms of our pact?

The answer is pretty obvious, especially to readers of the present narrative, which finally breaks the seal of silence that I put on the affair back in 1997.

But the essential thing is that the story didn't end with a simple bathetic return to "normality." Something came of it. Even though the ultimate descendants of the ADC—which no longer exits, of course, all of its functions having been dissolved into the Welsh Government in 2006, although its ghost doubtless still haunts the labyrinthine corridors of the Welsh Assembly—have never broken their own seal of secrecy, the work of exploration chemical analysis and testing for therapeutic effects of the alkaloids of the Glofeydd Diafol fungus must still be going on, quietly and methodically.

Even the experiments pioneered by Axel Castle and Claire Luchon might still be going on somewhere, even though they didn't get their research grant renewed, because the results of their first experimental run were so dismally unencouraging. After all, it really was an interesting idea, probably worth following up even if it didn't initially live up to youthful expectations, and it's not beyond the bounds of possibility that Penny spotted that, perhaps realizing the true value of my unappreciated contribution even from the second-hand account that Axel Castle gave her.

Alex never did sent me a copy of that Dictaphone tape, so it's perhaps as well that I still remember every word of it, in spite of its eccentric punctuation. I have to admit, though, that looking back at the accurate transcription I made of it in the last chapter, it could easily be mistaken by an unsympathetic observer for a load of meaningless gibberish, devoid of common sense. But what is there that has ever been written, throughout history, about the Cosmic Mind, or Him, or any of the other avatars thereof, that isn't vulnerable to exactly the same suspicion? That doesn't mean that we should stop trying to make the contact, and thus come up with a better understanding than the ones we've inherited.

All of which is, of course, only half an ending. It's the summation of what happened in the world at large as a result of the encapsulated adventure, but that's not the end of the personal story: the story of what happened to me as a result of my pact with the devil, and how it changed me—hopefully for the better, even though that implication would something of a reek of an upbeat ending about it, of which, as the Devil's advocate, I am bound to disapprove.

Superficially, in fact the change has hardly been noticeable, all the more so as people change routinely, especially as they get older, whether or not they get wiser. As the Devil so unkindly pointed out, mere human existence is discontinuous, fickle and unsteady as well as ephemeral, and it's always hard to determine whether any particular change was actually determined by a particular event or experience, or whether it would have happened anyway. People have a terrible tendency to take *post hoc propter hoc* arguments—the psychological basis of all superstition—far too seriously.

Even setting aside the possible effects of such mental pitfalls, though, I believe that meeting the Devil, supping with the Devil, and reaching an understanding with the Devil, really did make a difference to me, not merely to my light-mindedness, but, more importantly, to the substance and impetus of my dark mind. My obsessions have been refined, and I feel much more comfortable nowadays with my depression.

Neither of those things qualifies as mental illness, by the way, Obsessive Compulsive Disorder is only classified as such because the compulsive element to often leads to unproductive obsession. Voluntary obsession is the most orderly form of behavior there is, the very acme of sanity, especially on the part of a creative writer, even if hardly anyone actually reads his work. As for depression, anyone who isn't depressed in today's world is stark raving mad.

Nowadays, as a result of having met and made a pact with the Devil, I know certain things—important things—that I had never really brought to the surface of consciousness before, as a basis for rational evaluation and planning.

For one thing, I am now more firmly and completely committed than I ever was before to the idea that I should always bet the devil my head—which is I say that I always try to engage as seriously as possible with the antitheses of ideas that other people take for granted, that I should always be willing to stake my valuable time on the consideration of unconventional ideas, however absurd they might seem or ultimately turn out to be.

For another, I am now committed, as I was not previously, to the idea that one should never bet the Devil your heart, because that is definitely a game where the odds are far too heavily stacked for any person with an atom of sensitivity to have any change of winning. One of the most pervasive myths of modern culture, as exemplified in the fundamental narrative thrusts of modern fiction, is that if you follow your heart, things will work out in the end.

They won't, and anyone who clings to the conviction that they will, in spite of the evidence to the contrary, is a fool.

When Plato said that poets—meaning imaginative writers in general—ought to be expelled from the ideal Republic because they were engaged in the business of stimulating the wellspring of the emotions whereas rational men ought to be trying to drain it and seal it permanently, he might not have been entirely serious, but he did have a point. The rational man ought not to be a slave to emotion on principle, but also for the purely practical reason that if you allow your emotions to lead you, you will almost certainly end up, metaphorically speaking, in the ditch beside the road, all twisted and broken at the foot of a burning bike.

It was what the Devil told me in 1997 that persuaded me, with all the force of a conversion experience, that if I wanted to stay on the road—which is to say, if I actually wanted to get anywhere at all in life however meager that destination might turn out to be—then I ought to avoid investing my heart.

Have I lived up to that rule completely? Well, perhaps not—but I have tried, and trying has done me nothing but good. There's no point in going into detail, because I'm not trying to set any examples. I'm not preaching; I'm simply recording what happened, for the sake of the annals of human experience.

I often return to that room above Martin's bookshop, when I'm awake as well as asleep, and I always know, as soon as I step across the threshold, that I have been there a thousand times before and will return again. The books on the shelves are always dusty and uninteresting, even those not written in a foreign language, but it doesn't matter, because I don't go to browse the shelves; I go for the atmosphere, for the miasma. The Welsh Development Agency couldn't take that away from me, because once the link had been forged between my alternative states of consciousness, between the light mind and the dark, the fusion couldn't be undone, even though it didn't register on Alex Castle's EEG any more than the presence in the bookshop had registered on Penny's SPR machines.

The formal conditions of my pact with the Devil were satisfied long ago, but the exchange goes on between the sectors of my mind, and although the Devil doubtless still considers that he has the best of the unfair exchange, I'm not at all sure that I agree with him; value is, after all, a subjective matter, and I'm too well aware of the mediocrity of my soul to think that I can ever repay the Devil for what he has contrived to do for me, non-existent as he is. All in all, therefore, I believe that I came out of that room better than I went in on that first occasion, when I already remembered having been there before.

The most valuable thing that I've obtained from my pact with the Devil, however, isn't so much the content of the enlightenment that he offered me, when he was enabled to reach out briefly from the depths of dark mind with hands bearing gifts, but a finer appreciation of his method and, above all, his esthetics. Like Jesus, whom he admired so much, in spite of the fact that Jesus hadn't heeded his advice, the Devil taught by means of parables. He told stories. So do I.

I mentioned earlier in the plot having once heard A.N. Wilson give a talk about what he'd learned from writing his life of Jesus, and his conviction that the stream of consciousness is essentially a product of books. He argued, if I understood him correctly, that Jesus was essentially simple-minded and largely empty-headed, because he was not a reader, and therefore had not had the opportunity to have his mind shaped by literary discourse. I challenged him at the time by pointing out that the fact that Jesus taught by means of parables, and expected his listeners to understand the layers of meaning and the obliquity of his parables, strongly implied that both he and they were capable of much more sophisticated ways of thinking than A.N. Wilson seemed to believe.

The Devil confirmed that for me, with the added dimension of diabolism and subversion. Parables are, in fact, the very best way of cultivating esthetic sensitivity and constructing ethical principles, and they are, in consequence, the most hopeful means of subverting the esthetic sensitivities that have degenerated to the level of mere allergies and the ethical principles that have been twisted out of shape by the wear and tear of hypocrisy.

The Devil, seen in his true guise as an archetype of the collective unconscious, the reflexive antithesis of all bungled creation, can only work in mysterious ways, and the most effective of all those ways is by telling stories, not in a ritualized and formularistic way, but in perverse, ingenious and anarchic ways.

There is no guarantee of success if one does that, especially in the vulgar sense of making money or the slightly more pretentious sense of earning critical praise, but for those storytellers who follow their head rather than their heart, and bet with a modicum of common sense, the possibility of striking a chord somewhere in the vast wilderness of literate minds still remains, and still remains worthwhile.

Obviously, I could not have written this story if I had not met and made a pact with the Devil, and above all, I could not have supplied it with an appropriate ending.

Now I can, and I sincerely believe that I have.